Gun Lucky:
A Locked & Loaded Love Story

V. Mack Knight

Universal Unlimited Publishing--Detroit, MI
ISBN: 978- 0-9996943-1-2
Gun Lucky: A Locked & Loaded Love Story / V. Mack Knight
Available formats: eBook | Paperback distribution
2018

Other books by V. Mack Knight

How To Lose Weight On a Fast Food Diet by V.L. Jenkins

Gun Lucky: Never 2 Late For Love

Gun Lucky: Love V3ndetta

High Riders: Got Weed?

Chapter 1

Her innocent face was blank and emotionless, staring at her now ex-lovers cold corpse. Sharply her mind shifted back to one of the reasons he was now dead.

Underneath the bed in a small *attaché* case were supposedly seven million dollars worth of stolen Tokyo diamonds to be sold to a wealthy buyer in Las Vegas. Koji was to be in charge of the exchange and planned to fly out there this morning. His father was scheduling to come home that day from a business meeting with *his* masters in Japan.

Koji like herself was born American and also had a dangerous attitude that tested his father's authority to the point of spitting in his face. Luckily the young man had never roused his anger any more than slapping his face, if so than he would surely have killed him.

But this time he would find out, hopefully she thought after she'd gotten her hands on the money or worse case was left with a pretty box of jewelry.

She popped open the case with the key she found in the dead man's slacks breathing out a low, "Damn."

The sparkling diamonds were in a large black leather bag with a draw string, but next to it was a small Derringer pistol that had been constructed of solid platinum with a handle studded with large rare pink diamonds that had to make it worth a small country. Snapping out of her daze she slammed the case shut when a fist boomed against the door like thunder cracks.
The man at the door shouting excitedly in Japanese, which she understood perfectly was slamming his knuckles into the wood and shouting for Koji to open the door. Lotus searched the rest of the dead man's clothes on the chair finding a *Beretta* 92.

She picked the gun up nervously shaking a little. Killing a man with the poison was one thing while shooting one was entirely the opposite, extremely loud, very messy and took raw nerve.

The gun felt super heavy in her hands, like holding someone's past, present and future at the same time. She wondered if they would break the door down like in the movies or would she have the time or even the guts to shoot back when they did?

As the pounding and yelling became more urgent she made a split decision. Desperately rushing on her shoes she snatched up the case, creeping to the side of the door then slowly unlocking it.

As the door flew open a slim Japanese man in a cheap suit walked into the room expecting to be greeted by his boss, but instead was met with a swift kick to the balls that folded him like a Dear John letter.

"*Oomph*!" the gust of air escaping his lips barely made it out. His mouth was now cut from the swift kick Lotus planted on his kisser.

Reaching under his jacket for the *Browning* 9mm he had holstered, Lotus quickly finished him off with a chop to the back of his neck.

He dropped like an anvil to the floor finally managing to get the pistol out squeezing off a panic shot, but his target was long gone.

Outside the hotel parked across the street in a *Lincoln Continental* was Donnie *'Fingers'* Gianni a Mafia hitman for the Vittolo crime family in Queens. Donnie had been a part of the Mob his whole life starting out as a young kid running numbers to pulling hijacks out of *JFK Airport* to doing high profile hits for Bosses. It was said that the first time was always the hardest, but Donnie was a natural.

3

To this seasoned Mafia soldier whacking guys was almost as easy as whacking his *dick* and that's what most of the 20 plus he had killed were. These *Jap* punks, holding *their* stones were nothing... a walk in the sun.

"Shit, what the fuck's taking them so long, planes taking off soon?" he turned to his driver, Giuseppe '*Big Gus'* Falcone who frowned at the rhetorical question. The fat man had been with Donnie on at least 13 of those hits and knew the man was gifted at killing.

Donnie's' tone wasn't antsy, yet alone nervous, more like a man with a business appointment waiting for his client that was unacceptably late.

"Get ready to get out and grab the stones, kid once I tag him, you got that? I don't want to have to shoot up half this block... somebody tries to run off with them," he didn't have to finish. The kid in the back seat understood. Romero Ruggerio was the nephew of Mickey "*Twins*" Ruggerio, a man whom Donnie trusted with his life.

Mickey was now serving 10 years and Donnie had promised him that he would take care of the kid for him.

"Yeah sure thing Donnie, you got it," Romero shot back with the confidence of a seasoned soldier. This was his chance at a long career in one of the most respected families in New York and he wasn't about to fuck it up. Besides he wasn't the one pulling the trigger, this time.

"Oh shit it's the fucking broad!" Big Gus' announcement came out of nowhere. Donnie turned his attention to the sidewalk where Lotus was running top speed with the case in arm, holding a *Beretta* in plain sight.

The people walking to work that morning either didn't notice or didn't find the little Asian girl threatening, after all this was New York. In that moment the atmosphere changed dramatically as five Yakuza soldiers chasing her appeared from around the corner all brandishing large guns of their own.

"Fuck is you waiting for, permission or *somethin'*...?" Big Gus turned to Donnie who added a hand gesture to go with the order he gave his driver. He was now holding up the *Beretta Model* 12 sub-machine gun and tracking the Yakuza and Lotus as they ran down the block. Big Gus pulled into traffic catching up to them quickly, "Stay behind them, don't lose 'em!" Donnie spat the words viciously. That antsy feeling was coming over him again.

Lotus ran ducking into an alley as the shots fired behind her. She stumbled catching her balance, picking up her pace. More shots rang out as she stopped spontaneously turning to fire the Beretta.

It was something she thought she would never even be able to do, fire a gun and in an odd twist of fate she never did. The loud click she heard told her either she had done something wrong or the stupid thing just didn't work. She thought about dropping the useless thing, but for some strange unexplained reason she couldn't let go of it.

Gunfire lit up the block as Lotus turned to look back watching one of her Yakuza hunters drop. A *Lincoln* doing a drive-by shooting whipped up next to them unloading. This time the shots were rapid, nonstop and not aimed in her direction.

All the street vendors and early morning crowd on the street scattered in a panic leaving the Japanese soldiers in plain sight of the lethal Lincoln. Firing their hand guns two of them managed to shatter the back seat where Romero was left flinching from the flying glass.

"Get for the stones!" Donnie snapped as Big Gus peeled the big car down the long street.

The *Jap* broad had disappeared down one of the alleys, he knew to find her they'd have to bend some corners quick.

Lotus had managed to get away from the blue car chasing her by dipping around a corner into another alley, but she knew she had to keep moving. Steam rose from the manhole covers throughout the alleyway as she hid crouched behind an open dumpster. Sitting the case down, she quickly slipped the magazine from the useless pistol, *"Empty,"* that's what the problem was. There was something on the side of the clip that kept catching her eye, a bright sticker with an address printed on the top of it.

Chapter 2

Nicky Lee Cigarilli sat at the counter of his grandfathers' gun shop watching an old western movie on an old small RCA television. In the now classic scenario the squinty eyed nameless good guy was just about to blast the shifty eyed bad guy away for the umpteenth time.

Recognizing this scene he turned his attention back to the GLOCK 26 he was working on as he began to meticulously take the weapon apart. Usually the store manager, his friend Gino worked on the guns while Nicky either did inventory, worked the register or wrote down repair orders for Gino all day.

But this morning however, Gino had to take Maria his youngest daughter to the hospital and the guy who looked like a cop was supposed to be coming in to pick it up this morning. He knew how to fix guns, in fact he had a little side hustle going where he repaired guns for some of the guys he knew in the neighborhood. Life in the *Big Apple* was as real as it got and everybody these days needed protection even if the law didn't agree. He'd ran the shop before a few times, luckily for Nicky on those days no last minute repair pick-ups were ever scheduled, not to mention he'd still have to take it upstairs to the firing range to make sure it fired correctly.

Nicky was 18 years old, just graduated from high school and on his way up in the gunsmith business. He had learned how to fix guns at 15 when Gino who'd been working for his grandfather since Nicky could remember taught him everything he knew.

Nicky's' grandfather had come to America as an Italian immigrant kid in the 50's with his parents and had managed to turn the American dream into reality becoming a rich man in less than twenty five years and today he owned tons of business' and real estate all over New York City.

Nicky or '*Lucky*' as his grandfather had branded him once after finding a diamond ring on the beach in the sand as a boy, that he had gave to his widowed mother.

Nicky was a skinny kid with jet black hair, a clean baby face and intense eyes that added to the maturity of his look. At first glance he looked like some 13 year old kid, but one look into those eyes and you knew you were dealing with a man, not a boy.

Still working on the GLOCK Nicky looked up
when the bell to the front door went off and
trouble walked dead into his life,
"*Yo*? What can I do for you?"
"Is this yours?" Lotus slammed the gun on the
counter. Nicky picked up the *Beretta* 92,
"What's the problem with it?"
"It's empty..." she explained, "give me bullets for
this thing, okay...?" she rushed.
Nicky stared at her wearing a paralyzed
expression. This time she was more pressing,
"Do you understand English!"
"Yo, chill out... just give me a minute *alright*...
I'll get them for you in a second just hold..."

He stopped mid-sentence as the bell to the shop
went off yet again as four Japanese men holding
guns walked in.

"What the *fuck*?!" Nicky yelled as one of the men
replied by aiming his pistol. The window to the
gun shop shattered from the outside as the man
holding the gun immediately dropped from the
bullets now eating up the interior, "Shit!" Nicky
dropped behind the counter instinctively grabbing
the sawed off shotgun underneath there. The loud
explosions ceased as the bullets stopped flying
momentarily. Finally raising up he fired at the first
man that he saw holding a gun. The buckshot tore

11

the man's shoulder to bloody chunks as the last
two men turned their attention back towards the
counter. Nicky fired, hitting one of the men in the
face giving him a gruesome Hollywood horror
film makeover.

Two more shots rang out from the last mans'
Makarov 9-mm, as Nicky ducked down to the
floor. There he was met by Lotus who had
successfully managed to crawl behind the counter
to safety. She handed him the *Beretta*, this time the
clip was fully loaded.
"Thanks." Nicky snatched the gun as he heard
more shots cracking by. The last man alive in the
store continued to fire at the counter slowly
moving in for his kill. Nicky raised up and fired
nonstop leaving the man jerking back as he
stumbled over one of his dead brothers.

For a moment Nicky and Lotus took in the
destruction and death that had pierced the quiet
morning in a daze, then snapped out of it as more
shots came into the window forcing them to the
floor once more, "We got to get out of this place?!"
"Through there," Nicky pointed to the door for the
office work shop. Lotus crawled on her knees
reaching up opening the door. Nicky grabbed two
boxes of 9-mm shells from under the counter, got
to his feet then pulled her by the wrist like a child
playing in the street behind him. The door closed

behind them as Nicky pushed her in front of him, "Go!" He turned back for a second making sure no one was following them then looked back at Lotus noticing the large pink flower tattooed on her back. The tattoo was beautiful and reminded him of the ones he had seen on the backs of women in all those Japanese gangster movies he watched. "Come on!"

Nicky didn't hesitate to follow her words and before he knew it he was running down the alley with the Asian girl with the flower tattoo.

"Get in your car... come on, come on!" Donnie growled out the window as Big Gus pulled up to the bullet ridden gun shop where two Mafia soldiers were standing holding sub-machine guns. The gun shop was totaled, glass covered the floor and the sidewalk as well. Anyone inside had to be dead, "They ran out the back," one of the Mafia soldiers blurted.

"Get in...," Donnie waved his thumb out the window as the two men ran back for the *Buick* parked behind the Lincoln at the curb, jumping in guns still smoking, "Get to the alley," Donnie ordered and Big Gus sped around the block to cut the Japanese broad off.

"What the *fuck* is going on?"

"We're getting the hell up out of here, that's *what*."
Nicky wasn't satisfied with that answer, but knew
there wasn't time to argue with her. Right now the
guns were doing all the talking and he was sure
their conversation was far from over.

"Got car?" Lotus questioned, as she stopped to
look back at him,

"This way," Again Nicky grabbed her by the wrist,
leading her over to this old beat up *Toyota*. They
jumped into the rusty antique and the few seconds
it took for Nicky to get his keys in the ignition felt
like minutes. He finally got the car started and
was driving down the street a heartbeat later.

Donnie saw the car shoot out of the alley and
knew who it was from the near accident the little
piece of shit *Toyota* almost caused. "Follow it...," he
insisted. "They think they got away don't they, big
surprise," he was reloading the *Beretta Model* 12.

Nicky sped down the street as fast as traffic
would allow as screaming Blue and White squad
cars weaved through the oncoming lanes in the
opposite direction towards the gun shop. Seeing
this turned his thoughts from almost being killed
to why?

"So, you going to explain this shit to me or should I just turn around and go back?"

"'I wouldn't do that." she warned.

"Why?"

"Because you just murdered Koji Itoro, that's why."

"Who? I didn't *murder* anybody."

"You sure about that, did you get a good look back there...?"

Nicky was silent.

"Look, if you want to stay alive, you better stick with me."

"What do you mean if I want to *stay alive*, who the hell are you anyway?"

"Lotus... and all those guys were Yakuza. One was the son of Boss Kenji Itoro and when he finds out he died in your place, he'll come looking for you too."

Nicky didn't trust her, but there was something behind the warm brown eyes that said he probably could. The fact she was cute and had a tight ass only added to the indecisiveness he was feeling, "What the hell is that you got there anyway?" he growled,

"Let me get you a drink first, you're going need it."

Again Nicky was silent.

The interior of the strip club was damn near empty accept for a few guys on their lunch break. Lotus had picked the place and had Nicky park in the back where all the employees parked, just in case anyone had recognized his *Toyota*.

She knew the guy working at the back door and now they were seated in a corner booth close to the blaring speakers and far from the stage where a naked voluptuous young lady in a pink thong was swinging around the pole doing a routine that would earn her a shower of money, later on of course when the place became packed.

Lotus bounced in her seat to the music as Nicky sipped the cold Heineken beer. "You want another one?" Nicky ignored her as he sipped his beer, cool eyes to the stage.

"Oh, you want a lap dance...?" she questioned jokingly, sliding over next to him, "I could call her over here you want me too or I could just... give you one."

"You serious?"

"*Mm hmm.*"

"What the hell is this?" Nicky asked reaching under the table sitting the leather attaché case in front of him.

"The answer."

"To what?"

"All our problems."

16

Nicky was growing tired of her naughty girl routine and needed some real answers. The fact that four dead bodies were in his grandfather's gun shop didn't escape him. Lotus finally gave in to his intense stare, "O*kay*... it's seven million dollars in diamonds in that case and the buyer's in Las Vegas."

"Really...?"

Lotus nodded.

"And how'd you get'em?"

"They're mine," she bragged.

Of course that was bullshit and he smelled it, "Show me."

Lotus opened the case and gave him the bag. Nicky dug a hand in and came out with the kind of ice he knew didn't melt. He gave an involuntary whistle. Lotus smiled,

"See?"

"So, you're with the Yakuza? I thought they treated their women like shit,"

"Do I look like shit, to you?"

"*You*? Nah, you look like trouble,"

"And what do those look like?"

Nicky didn't have an answer to that one.

"Listen you go with me to the exchange, you know watch my back and I'll give you half. That way if you have any trouble with the cops you can just buy your way out of it,"

There was no denying it the diamonds were real. The glistening jewels were just as bright as the stage lights inside the pounding club. Lotus interrupted his thoughts, "Besides they don't know where we are anyway."

"You sure about that?"

"You still haven't told me your name or should I just call you..."

"Lucky," Nicky cut her off.

"*Lucky*...?" she giggled, "Do you believe in fate, Lucky?"

"Fate... that what that is?"

"*Yesss*...," she purred softly leaning in closer, rubbing her warm thighs up against him,
"Can't you see it? Here I am, going to Las Vegas and who do I meet... a cutie named, *Lucky*... it has to be."

"And almost getting our heads blown the fuck off, that a part of it too?"

She reached for the empty bottle in his hand, "Here, let me get you another one."

Chapter 3

Detective Richard 'Dick' Benedict drove into the Itoro Estate in his navy blue *Crown Victoria* thinking about the crime scene he had just witnessed at the gun shop. The four stiffs belonged to Itoro and word that his son had been found in a hotel not too far from the place meant this meeting with the Yakuza boss wasn't going to be a pleasant one.

The 20 plus years he had been a New York cop were filled with corruption, that he justified by telling himself he was playing referee for the cities syndicates. When he pulled up to the Yakuza house he saw some of Itoro's soldiers standing in front of the place like *Buckingham Palace*.

The sight of all those stone faced *Japs* made him jittery, so he nervously removed his flask then took a hefty swallow. He parked in front got out walking up only to be greeted by a stiff palm to the chest that would have knocked him off balance had the pouch he called his stomach not weighed him down.

"*Hey*, you know who the fuck I am? Somebody educate this asshole!" The order fell on deaf ears as the man began to search the Detective almost as professionally as Benedict himself. The man removed his *Smith & Wesson* No.29 44 Magnum and Benedict reacted by grabbing his wrist. Every Yakuza soldier blindingly drew his pistol with the speed of a seasoned samurai pulling out a razor sharp katana blade.

"*Hey*! You want me to send a squad down here and have each and every one of you sushi eating sons of bitches deported? Boss Itoro is expecting me, so run and tell him the *New York Police* is here!"

"Dead men do not make phone calls,"
Benedict looked to the voice and saw a tall, fat Japanese man in a white kimono with a red sash wrapped around it. Boss Itoro had been in the doorway watching his men intimidate the policeman and had found his nervousness quite amusing.

He gave rapid orders in Japanese and his men holstered their weapons as fast as they had drew them respectfully bowing.

Benedict copied them with the S&W, adjusted his neck tie and entered the house, he'd be damned if he bowed.

The interior of the house was like stepping across the Pacific Ocean furnished with traditional furniture, exotic Masaki plants, beautiful Spirea flowers and scroll like wall paper written in ancient Japanese script, with pictures of crane birds. A few men followed them in, but when they reached the main room in the back Itoro signaled them with a wave of a hand to wait outside as he and Benedict entered his private area.

Inside the room was a small office where Itoros' accountant was taking care of some important paper work, but when he was signaled to leave the thin well-dressed Asian man adjusted his glasses, bowed humbly and swiftly left the room.
Johnny '*Flash*' Tanaka who was the boss's personal bodyguard did not leave. His hard squint watched Benedict, like a hawk waiting for a precise moment to strike. His face was a blank slate giving nothing away and was topped off with jet black hair that had a short dyed Mohawk. The red highlights were symbolic of Johnny's' fiery streak and infamous hot headed temper.
The silk suit he wore made the Detective feel like the one he'd worn might as well have been rags. The thought filled him with contempt.

"I just left a crime scene in Queens that had your name written all over it. You've got a pretty big fuck up on your hands and in order for me to

cover things up this time, I'm going to need a nice advance to spread around, you know what I mean?" Itoro sat in his comfortable plush leather chair and leaned back a little as he listened, "I think *50* grand should keep things quiet... for now," as Benedict finished Itoro's silent penetrating gaze prompted him to continue, "Also about your son, I heard he was with..."
"The devils detective! That is where he is now, *Hell* for his betrayal of his Master...," Itoro rapidly snapped, his lips curled up in a snarl adding, "and as far as your cover-up, your results thus far have been proven ineffective," As Benedict listened Johnny shifted a little behind him. Noticing out of the corner of his eye he felt himself grow slightly nervous from the movement, "Where is she?!" Itoro barked.
"She?" Benedict turned his thoughts back to their conversation,
"Lotus... the cause of all my trouble this grievous morning," Benedicts' tension eased a little as he remembered what he was in the middle of telling the Yakuza boss,
"The girl?" Itoro nodded indicating for the policeman to continue, "Right now I don't know, but you give me 24 hours and I'll definitely have something on her."

Nicky opened his eyes and found himself on top of a bed with Hello Kitty covers and pillows. The bedroom looked like it could have belonged to a little girl judging from the teddy bears he shared the bed with and the giant stuffed Hello Kitty sitting in the small chair in the corner. His head was pounding like the speakers in the club as he sat up noticing he was only dressed in his boxer shorts. Nicky groaned as he sat up eyes spinning, one too many he thought as his hangover reminded him.

"He lives," Lotus was now in the doorway still in her bra and panties smiling at him,

"Where are we?" Nicky asked groggily.

"My place."

"Where's my clothes?" Lotus pointed to the corner opposite Hello Kitty and Nicky saw his pants and shirt on the floor. He got up and quickly slipped his pants back on,

"Don't worry, I only peeked a little," she confessed.

"What?"

Lotus giggled, "You want some coffee?"

"I *want* some answers,"

"Okay, shoot," Lotus held her hands together then pointed two fingers at him mockingly.

"Funny... where you keep yo' phone at?"

"Kitchen,"

"And the gun...?"

Lotus walked to the dresser and grabbed the *Beretta*, handing it to him.

"Thanks,"

"You're welcome," Nicky quickly slipped the clip from the pistol and checked the magazine, two bullets remained. He dug in his pants pocket and pulled out the box of 9mm shells then loaded the clip. He then cocked the weapon removed the magazine then filled it back to the tip.

"I love your tattoo," Lotus admitted as she began massaging his shoulders. Her soft touch eased some of his tension, relaxing him,

"Yours ain't too bad," Nicky replied.

Like Lotus he also had a large tattoo across his back. Two large gold revolvers crossed his shoulder blades with the words 'BAD ASS' written in a ribbon underneath. Nicky slapped the clip in with a stiff palm.

Outside of Lotus' apartment building trouble was waiting. Jimmy 'Ice Pick' Pezzo was sitting in a clean four door *Cadillac* with three of his goons all armed to the teeth. Four more guys who were strictly backup were parked two cars back in another clean *Caddy*.

The *Jap* broad and the kid from the gun store were up on the fifth floor in room 525.

That information had come from the maintenance manager who was probably on his way to the emergency room after the vicious beating Bobby 'Bare Knuckles' Verdone had given him earlier. When Elmo Fox was first cornered by the gangsters sometime around 5:30 am, he had just began his morning clean up and repair duties. The little, short old man had managed to put up a fight even swinging a wild fist at his attackers. After Bobby struck him in the head with a few hard jabs and an unforgiving uppercut that would have floored the heavyweight champ. Immediately the marks attitude changed from temperamental to timid. After that the words flowed from his mouth like the man had sprung a leak. Jimmy then told the guy to beat it for at least four hours adding that if he went to the cops he'd wind up in the Hudson River, by morning. Now all that remained was going upstairs, taking them out and grabbing the stones... a slice of cake, "You boys ready...?" The men in the car expressed their agreements then Jimmy added, "Then let's go already."

Nicky was on the cell phone in the hall watching Lotus slip into a white dress. When she finished adjusting her dress in the mirror, she removed her panties and she didn't go for another pair.

Nicky involuntarily licked his lips then hung up the phone. She slid up next to him,

"So, she home...," Lotus asked quietly.

Nicky looked into her almond brown eyes,

"Your girlfriend, *right*?"

His mother didn't answer her phone, he briefly thought about calling Gino at the gun shop, but he knew he didn't have the answers to all the questions he or cops would be asking.

"Is that how you normally go out?" he pointed below her waist.

"Why, you like it like that?"

"Hey, baby if you like it I love it, but I'll bet your man don't,"

"You're right, he doesn't...," she moved in kissing close continuing, "but he's not here, is he?" she whispered softly in his ear.

"So, when's he coming back?"

"He's not, I share this place with a girlfriend,"

"Girlfriend?" Nicky's' eyebrows rose intriguingly as he noticed a picture of a blonde girl sitting on the shelf. Lotus nodded slowly. Again he wet his lips as she went in to kiss him when a swift kick snapped the apartment door open, but the chain lock stopped it. This time a burly shoulder finished the job as a goon entered the room grunting from the doors impact. Lotus reacted by running back into the apartment to her bedroom.

Nicky reacted, aiming the *Beretta* then firing at the man. The thug made a slight cry of pain as his head snapped back from the hot slug that connected just above the bridge of his nose. Dropping his *Desert Eagle* he fell to the floor spraying blood in the face of the mobster who was following him into the apartment.

Nicky squeezed the trigger and caught the man in the arm that held the SIG-Sauer P226 which he lost in the pain that followed.

Nicky slid behind the wall to the kitchen as holes were punching through it from more raging rounds. A third man entered firing blindly down the apartment hall then ran inside. Nicky fired from around the corner hoping to finish the last guy off. The silence that followed told him that he hadn't succeeded.

As Nicky sat behind the stove the thug crept into the dining area looking for him. Lotus ran up and kicked the gangster in his side knocking him into the small dining room table, he fell into it flipping it over.

Nicky saw Lotus run pass him, when he heard the commotion he lifted himself to his feet aiming at the man who was scrambling to get to his. The bullets hit him in the throat and the final shot he got off missed Nicky smashing a glass pitcher that was sitting on top of the counter top.

"You okay?"

Lotus managed to nod as she quickly ran up wrapping her shaking self around him. He felt her warm breath as she panted a little. A shot discharged and Nicky reacted by collapsing on top of her finishing off the *goombah* he had forgot about with the SIG. The slugs hit him in the face and this time the pistol dropped from his hand forever. Springing to their feet, Nicky retrieved the dead man's *Desert Eagle* then peeked into the hallway, it was empty.

Jimmy the '*Ice Pick*' heard the shots and knew he had heard too many. He was standing next to his *Cadillac*, "Get the fuck up there," he shouted as Bobby 'Bare knuckles' led three more guys into the building.

Lotus just stared at the cadavers expressionlessly, "You know these guys?"

"Yeah," she admitted quietly.

"Well?"

"They're Mob guys."

"Mob guys?"

"You know, *Mafia*?"

"Oh yeah, I know, but how do they know you?"

"They don't."

"Looks like they do. We got to get out of here...!"

Lotus ran back into her bedroom,
"Did you just hear me, we're talking about the
Mafia here? If we don't leave now, we're *not*
leaving!" Nicky ran back in to grab her once more,
but Lotus met him in the hall where she slammed
a small gym bag into his chest. Nicky held the bag
as Lotus sprinted out the apartment door with the
diamond case.
"Well, we leaving or staying?" Lotus asked
sarcastically. Nicky put every gun inside the
apartment into the gym bag then threw the strap
over his shoulder trailing her down the hall. As
they ran down the hallway and got closer to the
elevator they heard.
"There they are!" The voice sounded frantic. Two
Italian looking guys were entering the hall from
the staircase, dressed just like the ones that were
dead on Lotus' apartment floor,
"Forget it... the stairs!" Nicky pulled Lotus by the
arm as they ducked into the exit door next to the
elevator.
    They hit the stairs at top speed getting two
flights down when the door they entered opened
behind them. Two gangsters gave chase as five
shots chewed into the wall below. Nicky yanked
Lotus close to him. More shots came that were
intended to keep them both pinned down.

Nicky peeked up holding the Desert Eagle he had lifted from one of the dead men earlier then squeezed a shot. The huge round burst the goon's knee and left him tumbling down the steps yelling in agony. The guy behind him fired in Nicky's direction, leaving him and Lotus dashing from the gunfire.

They were now one floor from the exit when the door opened abruptly. Nicky aimed over Lotus' shoulder but hesitated seeing an old man oblivious to the gunfight staring in shock at the deadly weapon in the young man's hand.

The old man was deaf and when a shot went off behind them he didn't budge. Nicky spun and fired nonstop through the staircase above as a loud grunt of pain from the last gangster let him know that the man was now just above them. The last two heavy rounds penetrated the thin metal and completed the job. Nicky heard his pistol clatter down the steps. Creeping up he saw the body and the large exit wounds in his torso. He added the man's handgun, a *Smith & Wesson Model* 410 to his collection. The old man stood motionless in the doorway. Lotus found her feet removing her hands from her ears,
"Come on!" Nicky yelled. She noticed he was heading back up the stairs,
"You crazy? We got to get out of here, *remember*?"

"We are, but not that way,"

"What?!"

"They're waiting for us outside too,"

"Then, how?"

"Through the apartment."

When they got back in the apartment Nicky ran over to the window looking down towards the street. He opened it then crawled onto the fire escape quickly helping Lotus out. They hurried down to the alley below without any trouble then they both jumped down a few feet from the hanging ladder. Nicky went first then Lotus tossed him the case. She jumped down landing into his arms. He scanned the alley, but no one had spotted them.

"Come on," she said rushing off down the alley,

"The car's the other way," Nicky complained as Lotus went off in the opposite direction.

"Then we'll just have to get another one, won't we?" Lotus ran into the parking lot as Nicky jogged behind her stopping at an old beat down *Chrysler* minivan, "Like it?" she asked as she opened the unlocked tailgate. Nicky scanned around again to see if they were being followed.

Lotus crawled over the seats and was now under the dashboard with a switchblade. Nicky wondered just where she had hidden it given her limited choice of clothing.

The minivan engine growled to life as she crawled behind the steering wheel. When she unlocked the passenger side door Nicky jumped in, "Let's get the hell out of this city. Get on the 278 west, take it to the *Verrazano*."

"Just tell me the way,"

"You *can* drive... can't you?"

Lotus flashed a wicked smile then jerked the shift into drive. The back windshield suddenly was smashed as bullets flew into the minivan from the end of the alley. A single man stood there firing a large pistol. Lotus put the *Chrysler* in reverse, mashed the pedal and zoomed directly at him as a second man appeared blasting a MP5KA1 that ripped through the minivan cracking the windshield then shattering it.

Nicky leaned out of the window firing both the *Beretta* and the *Desert Eagle*. His shots spun Jimmy the *Ice Pick* around like a top ending the man's life long career with the Mafia.

Stumbling Bobby 'Bare knuckles' dove to the side of the moving vehicle and was clipped by the minivan. His ankle was crushed under the back tire. During the impact he lost the MP5KA1 grabbing for his shattered talus bone instead. Lotus spun the minivan around into the street, slammed it into drive then accelerated away.

Chapter 4

Richard Benedict hated his nickname. It all started when he was just a kid, when his alcoholic father started mockingly calling him Dickie. In grade school it only got worst and those kids that teased him didn't start receiving bloody noses until the eighth grade. So when the Police Captain occasionally reminded him of his childhood torment with his slick comments, he fumed and had to physically restrain himself from kicking his ass all over the station and furthermore jeopardizing his pension. Itoro had made his job easy telling him exactly where the Japanese girl was going. Las Vegas was always nice this time of year and he had no doubts that if she was there, he would find her. The boy 'Nicky' had still not been heard from and was most likely still with her. He'd found out the young man's name from the greasy haired guy who ran the gun store when he visited the crime scene earlier just after the shootout. He also had gotten as much info on

Itoro's involvement as he could. He took a swallow of whiskey and briefly wondered if he was walking into a trap. His relationship with the Japanese gangster had been on the rocks as of late and the man was smart enough to know that he had more than enough to put him away for two lifetimes. Those thoughts of worry swiftly passed as the expensive liquor took effect.

He knew he'd see anything of that sort coming a mile away and the seven million in diamonds, if there were any was worth the risk. He glanced at his watch, he had a plane to catch.

Nicky sat on one of the twin beds inside the small motel somewhere in *Jersey*. He stared at the phone seriously thinking about calling someone, but knew the truth was that no one he knew could help him out this late in the game.

He was definitely in it for the long ride now and getting to the money was his best bet at staying alive and out of prison. He looked at the *Remington* 12 gauge shotgun that sat next to him, it was the latest addition to his collective. How he'd acquired the scatter gun still played out in his head like some summer action movie sequence.

They had successfully made it out of the city as they planned. After trading the *Dodge* minivan for a *Ford* station-wagon Lotus had stopped at a small town gas station and decided they needed a little bit more than just a fill-up.

She held the place up at gunpoint, stolen the man's shotgun then got the two of them into a high speed chase that had almost gotten them killed. An oncoming semi that barely missed them ending up hitting the police car that had chased them from the gas station instead. The girl clearly was un-bottled trouble.

"You know, we only needed *one* bed," Lotus cracked.

Nicky lost his train of thought looking pass her turning on the TV sitting on top of the wooden dresser. He then sat on the first bed reaching for the remote control, "*Hellooo*, sexy girl, right here...," she announced waving her hands in his face, pointing to her chest.

Nicky was flicking through the channels oblivious looking for any news on the last two wildest days of his life.

"So you're going to ignore me now?"

Nicky looked at Lotus then back towards the TV,

"We'll see how long that last," she teased walking towards the bathroom removing the dress, her naked frame disappearing into the door. Nicky's eyes flickered in her direction just in time to see her vanish into the bathroom.

Shower water ran as the door closed. He finally found a news cast on *Channel 14* that had something on a shootout in Queens, but he had missed the names and details or maybe they just didn't have any he hoped.

Lotus was in the bathtub taking a hot shower, singing a love song in Japanese. Nicky turned the TV down to listen. He didn't understand the words, but noted the light warm heartedness in her tone. She sounded as if she had just had the two happiest days of her life.

The water abruptly stopped and a few seconds later she stepped from the bathroom wearing a towel wrapped around her wet body. The TV was now turned off and as she cut the bathroom light off the room went black. Walking up to the bed Nicky was sprawled across, she slowly began massaging his shoulders tenderly. She let the moist towel droop from her body effortlessly and continued rubbing, "You know, I think all you need to do... is relax your mind, listen to your heart and let...," Nicky's snoring got louder, "*fate*... do its part," sighing she sat on the other bed staring at him.

When the bathroom light went out in the motel room Donnie got out of his *Fleetwood Cadillac*, "Gus watch the door, come on, kid,"

Romero got out of the back seat following Donnie towards the motel office. They had followed the two brats in the stolen car all the way into New Jersey and when the station-wagon had almost been hit by the semi-truck Donnie thought they might lose the jewels. When the station-wagon finally parked at the motel he decided they'd make their move when the two of them went to sleep.

"May I help you?" the old man with the pot-belly and granddaddy glasses asked from behind the counter looking irritated. Donnie had no time for small talk he was anxious to get to the jewels and he responded by walking behind the counter and gun-butting the old man breaking his glasses and busting his nose.

Attaching a silencer to the GLOCK 26 he pointed it at the elderly mans blood streaked face, "Take it! Take everything," the old man's blurted in absolute terror pointing to the cash drawer, "Get up," Donnie commanded as the old man quickly lifted himself up by the counter. He hit the button on the register causing the cash drawer to fly open as he quickly began gathering up the money inside. Donnie leaned the gun on his arm as he held the money up,
"Keep it, just give me the key to the room you gave the kid and the broad."

The old man dug under the counter and Romero cocked the hammer on his *Browning High Power* 9-mm. The chilling sound made the old man hesitate then he slowly came up with a spare key to room 109,

"Give me your phone," Donnie ordered and the old man came out of his pocket with a *Motorola* cell-phone that he tossed to the gangster. Donnie nodded to Romero who viciously yanked the desk top phone from out of the wall, slamming the unit on the floor cracking it open. After he briefly explored the little office space Donnie was convinced there was no other way out of there, "Lock the door and stay in here 'till morning, that way you might live to see the sun. I see you again tonight and," Donnie finished his statement by raising the silenced weapon. The man nodded as Romero searched under the counter removing a No. 2 *Smith & Wesson* 0.38 caliber revolver. Romero shook the ancient pistol mockingly at the old man as he and Donnie exited.

Across the parking lot Big Gus watched out for any witnesses. When Donnie and Romero walked back up to the Cadillac he rolled down the window and asked, "What's up?"

"We got the key. Watch the office, you see that old prick in there come out whack him. Keep the car running..." Donnie insisted.

Big Gus nodded his understanding,
"let's go," Romero fell in step following Donnie
towards room 109. The door to room 109 opened
without a sound and light coming from the lamps
outside through the window made out the shape
of the beds and the furniture. The *Jap* broad was
on one bed and the gun store kid was on the other.
The sight of this made Donnie smile in the
darkness. Creeping towards the desk in between
the beds he lifted the *Beretta* there and handed the
pistol over to Romero.

Donnie was now seated in the lone chair in the
room near the foot of the bed Lotus was sleeping
in. Pulling out a large cigar he sparked his *Zippo*
lighter twice as he began puffing on the stogy.

Nicky heard the sound and reacted a split
second too slow reaching for the desk, nothing
was there. Before he had dozed off he had sat the
gun down right there, he knew it. The duffel bag
was still in the car and he briefly wished that he
had at least brought one more gun with him.

The lights came on as Romero flipped the
switch waking Lotus as well. Startled she looked
at the man in the chair smoking a cigar, then to the
young man standing by the door. They looked
Italian so that meant the Mafia had found them,
but how?

"How you doing baby?" Donnie asked. Lotus ignored him looking at Nicky who was staring at the *Beretta* in Romero's hand, the same one he had just reached for.

"Something wrong, kid...?" Donnie questioned sarcastically. Nicky didn't answer. Jokingly Fingers continued, "What's with this...," he pointed back and forth from Nicky to Lotus, "You shooting blanks or something?"

Romero began to snicker. Walking over to the side of Lotus' bed he grabbed her by her hair, yanking her from under the covers exposing her petite naked body. Growing furious at the sight of this, this punk with his gun Nicky jumped from the bed forcing Donnie to fire a single shot from the silenced GLOCK 26 into the pillow leaving a visible burning hole through it. Nicky stopped his rush to face the gangster,

"Now that I got your attention... let's get down to business..." Donnie suggested turning back to Lotus, "where's the stones?"

"They're in your head," was her response.

"Cute...," Donnie laughed removing a cigar cutter that he began snapping loudly, "Alright one last time, tell me where the diamonds are or I start chopping off your pretty little fingers one by one...," he warned. Lotus just glared at him, "Or maybe I should just shoot your new

40

boyfriend. What you think about that...?" Donnie barked then asked, "*Huh*, huh?!" The GLOCK 26 lifted as Nicky braced himself for the bullets impact,
"Black case, in the car," Lotus blurted it out. Lowering the gun Donnie beamed,
"*Right*, I knew that..." Looking at Nicky he barked, "Well don't just sit there fuck face, get moving..." Turning to Romero he instructed, "Take him out there and get Gus,"
Romero looked into Nicky's burning eyes and saw the rage and anger brewing there. He let Lotus' hair go then walked up to Nicky barking,
"Move it shithead," He led Nicky out the motel room at gun point. Donnie turned his attention from the closing door back towards Lotus,
"Alone at last."

"Two beds...," Romero let out a laugh then continued, "What the hell's wrong with you huh, you *homo* or some shit...?" Romero shoved the gun barrel roughly between Nicky's shoulder blades. "Tell me you hit that? You had to... I know I would have," Romero finished. When they got to the car Gus asked Romero, "What's Donnie doing in there, why is he still alive?" he pointed to Nicky.
"He's getting the stones from the car, so get off your fat ass and come on,"

Romero led Nicky across the lot and Gus got out following them, "Hey you little, *jag* off wait up,"

Stopping at the driver side door of the station wagon Nicky dug inside his pants pocket, "*Hey*..!" Big Gus held his *Smith & Wesson* No. 38 9-mm revolver directly to Nicky's head, "Don't move...," Gus frisked him as quickly as his free hand allowed then backed away, "Fuck are you reaching for?" he asked suspiciously, "The *keys*," Nicky answered sarcastically. "Better be..." Gus warned, "Watch him," he ordered Romero as his eyes wandered the parking lot for onlookers. Romero got behind Nicky and put his own *Beretta* to the back of his head, "Come on cocksucker! Get it open," Romero barked as a young woman pushing a cleaning cart slowly came out from one of the rooms, "Hold it," Gus advised as the woman obliviously moved the cart two doors down opening the room. Just then a woman and man came from out of there room into the parking lot laughing and talking loudly. As the two mobsters turned their attention towards the couple Nicky speared Romero in the gut knocking his wind from him. Romero gasped doubling over clutching at his stomach. Nicky jammed the sharp key deep into Romero's right eye, as far as he could. For a brief sickening moment they dangled from his bloody socket then clanked to the ground. Pain shot through the young gangster's brain like a lightning bolt as he reached for his gory retina, grunting and moaning. Gus reacted by firing a shot at Nicky who ducked just in time as the window to the station wagon burst from the bullets. Ramming into Romero he knocked him into the fat man throwing Big Gus off balance. As another shot hit the back window of the station wagon Nicky dived over the hood and falling to the ground sliding back up against the fender. Gus turned his gun towards the man and woman as they ran back for their motel room. He didn't fire in their direction instead cautiously creeping around the back of the vehicle looking for Nicky, "Shit," When he got to the other side of the car he didn't see the little bastard.

Romero grunted louder as Gus waddled over to him. Blood was dripping from his eye and he was in a fetal position clutching at his head. Big Gus scanned the interior of the car with his eyes then stuck his arm in the shattered driver side window. He popped the lock, yanked the door open then started searching frantically,
"Where the fuck are they? Aaah, *shit!*"
A gunshot rang out from under the car as
Big Gus' left foot exploded from a bullet from
Nicky's recovered *Beretta*. The big man dropped

squeezing off a panic shot underneath the car. Nicky was now running across the parking lot and heading back for Lotus in the motel room. Gus fired three more shots in his direction missing again as Lotus ran up kicking the revolver flying out of his hand, following it up with a kick to the fat man's face that snapped his head back like a gunshot. She carried the diamond case in her arms and was totally in the buff,

"Ready for that lap dance *now*...?!"

Nicky tilted his head curiously at her as she yelled, "Let's go, lucky boy!"

Yanking open the driver door Nicky picked the bloody car keys up off the ground,

"I'm gon' kill you, you little prick!" Romero painfully promised. Nicky kicked him in the stomach then got in the car cranking the engine as Lotus crawled into the passenger door,

"Where's the other one?"

"*He wanted* more than a lap dance... instead I gave him the phone," Nicky looked at her confused as she smiled cruelly. Without a second thought he put the car in drive then peeled out of the parking lot.

Chapter 5

Morgan Anna Le Beau was a special child born with an incredible gift that she didn't even began to fully understand until her late teenage years. At first she took the multiple visions she had as no more than just daydreaming, until the day she had the one of her mother's death in an automobile accident. The fear of her family not believing her had convinced her to hide her car keys to prevent this.

She turned out to be right as a pile up of vehicles on Interstate 10, the route which her mother normally took to pick her father up from work had left at least 8 people dead. She then took her ability to foresee events to the streets of New Orleans giving good folks lucky lottery numbers, and telling futures, for a small fee of course.

Later Morgan started using her extraordinary talents helping the local law enforcement solve cold cases, winning her national recognition in the media and landing her recent job as host to 'The Mystical *Morganna in the Morning'* show.

The live television broadcast had been on air for four years and counting and was usually top five in weekly ratings, even earning Morganna an Emmy award for best daytime talk show hostess.

She was having a pomegranate juice backstage in her dressing room at WPHL studios in Philadelphia, PA waiting for her set manager Charles to signal her return to the stage when she abruptly had one of her visions.

When they first came she would feel a splitting headache followed by nausea then passing out. Now they felt more like an intense throbbing that immediately passed.

The images were rapid and blurred with glimpses of clarity. In it she saw a young Asian girl, then a large pink flower. A young man was shooting a gun at men that appeared to be protected in black armor. The images came suddenly and intense when a loud knock on the door came without warning,

"Morganna in five," Charles yelled through the door.

Morganna looked into the mirror and saw a beautiful smooth face with light caramel complexion skin highlighted by high cheek bones, small pouty lips and hazel colored eyes that held a hint of mystery to them. Her long sandy brown hair was wrapped up in a colorful scarf that represented the many colors of her family's island roots all over it. She cut the fan on then fired up a marijuana cigarette.

"Three, two, one...," the set director announced as the cameras began the live feed of the 'Mystical Morganna in the Morning' show. She was now back on stage sitting in a comfortable, plush cream sofa.

The set was a modest powder blue design with tarot cards painted all over in a decorative fashion. Her guest had a couch to sit on, but her current guest was on the phone, it was now the call in portion of the show.

"Morganna in the mooooor-niiiiing,"
Came in through the speakers in a harmonic sing song tone, "Welcome back everyone to 'Morganna in the Morning'. I'd like you all to welcome my next guest... caller you're now on the air with Morganna and with whom do I have the pleasure of speaking?"

Nicky opened his eyes and saw open road and extensive grassland running along the Interstate. When he regained his focus he turned to Lotus who was on her cell phone, "Hell's the matter with you, how you think they keep finding us...?"

Nicky snatched the cellphone from the side of her head tossing it out of the window as if it was a live grenade, "They're tracking us, can't you see that?" he asked leaning back in his seat,

"Thanks for being an *asshole* this morning," she countered.

"You're welcome,"

"Next caller, you're on the air...," on the radio Morganna sighed adding, "Now, Niccolo, why'd you gone and do that for?"

Nicky was in the middle of loading one of his guns when the mention of his birth name drew his attention like gunfire,

"What did she just say?" he was cut off as Lotus turned the radio up louder.

"Little impatient this morning isn't he?" Morganna asked. Lotus nodded her head answering,

"Yes, he is,"

Turning his attention between Lotus and the radio Nicky felt like he was in the middle of a conversation that was all about him,

"Don't worry, Flower Girl, I'm a see y'all in a lil' bit… next caller?" Morganna promised.

Lotus turned the radio back down and ignored Nicky's confused stare.

"What the hell just happened?" he wondered aloud. Lotus just smiled at him,

48

"You don't know who Mystical Morganna *is*?" she focused on the road.

"*Who*... are you talking 'bout that psycho chic on TV?"

"It's not psycho… it's *psychic*, smart ass,"

Nicky grinned, "You actually believe that fortune cookie *shit*?"

"You have to believe in something,"

"Oh I do, I believe you're crazy. How 'bout pulling over, get us something to eat?"

"You can *eat*, this," Lotus shot back holding up her middle finger.

Pulling into the truck-stop Lotus cut the engine then turned to face Nicky's angry face,

"So, Lucky... are you going to be a good boy when you come in with me or should I just bring out a doggy bag?" Ignoring her slick talk he got out and walked straight through the diner doors,

"Good boy," Lotus teased as she followed him in.

Philadelphia International Airport.
Philadelphia, PA

Detective Benedict sat in the lobby looking at the flight schedule, "Shit," He'd been here for five hours already for some silly delay with the plane and just his luck turned out they were also having fueling problems too. He bit down his rising anger and went back to reading his *USA Today*.

49

Philadelphia International was packed with travelers and staff. The place was swarming with security, the very reason Nicky had chosen to leave the platinum & diamonds Derringer behind. They would be gone less than a week and he was sure that they'd have the money by then. Lotus argued she wasn't leaving it when Nicky promised her they would come back for it.

Once inside, Nicky made sure to look straight ahead, not making eye contact with anyone. When they got to the metal detector he kept as cool as the *ice* in his underwear. Walking through, heart pumping, palms moist he anticipated problems. The only thing that followed was Lotus who came through as well without any trouble, so far so good.

When Benedict got up to go back to the counter and question the young woman there he was greeted with a warm smile that unarmed some of his aggression, "Hi, sir, may I help you?" her words were friendly and full of spunk. Benedict's lips twitched in response as he handed her his ticket,

"How much longer?" the detective inquired agitated. Her fingers ran over the *Dell* computers keyboard like working insects. She looked up the bright smile returning, "Not long, sir,"

Nicky and Lotus walked pass the ticket counter where Benedict was now fuming,
"If we get recognized in here?" Nicky didn't finish, his silence ended his statement,
"This was your idea. I wonder what's happening over there?" Lotus asked extending a fingernail towards the crowd that was coming up just in front of them. Nicky searched the throng with cool eyes, people seemed to be surrounding one person. Without a word Lotus walked off into the crowd,
"*Hey*... get back here!" Nicky gave chase shoving his way through the mass of people. When he finally got to the center he saw who it was being surrounded. He recognized the African American woman in the traditional Caribbean clothing with the colorful head wrappings as she signed autographs. Morganna looked up to face Nicky and Lotus, "So, tell me now, now you ready to listen to what I got to say?"

As they walked her towards the boarding dock Morganna told them their future,
"Now listen, you two are putting yourselves in more danger than you can possibly imagine,"
"I'll go get the tickets," Nicky suggested turning to walk away,
"Niccolo?" Morganna's words pierced Nicky's soul as he turned around dumbfounded.

The psychics beautiful smile and eyes were full of confidence, "What you just call me?"

"The name yo' sweet momma *gave' ya...*," Morganna continued, "now, you got more than just gangsters to worry about."

"Who else?" Nicky asked, questioning her with a hard gaze.

"Evil... evil in the form of men with intentions and power beyond comprehension,"

"What should we do?" Lotus sounded concerned.

Nicky smirked, he had to hold in his laughter.

"Follow your hearts, listen to your feelings, and then wait."

"For what?" Nicky asked skeptically.

"The call... of fate...," Morganna spread her arms up high and wide adding drama to her advice. Nicky just shook his head, "Here, take this," Morganna handed Lotus a copy of her best-selling book on the tarot, "There, you'll find a passage inside that will lead you to... *higher* enlightenment to the darkness ahead," Morganna promised holding Lotus' hand.

"Which one?" Lotus wondered.

"You'll know when you find it, child. *Oh*, and one more thing..." Lotus waited for the tarot reader to finish, "Don't take the plane."

After Morganna boarded her plane she took her seat in first class ordering a *Dole* pineapple juice. Shortly after the air bus took off and they were all finally airborne. Morganna leaned back in her seat closing her eyes. A few moments of peace gave way to a sudden violent vision of Las Vegas, NV. People appeared decapitated and torn limb from limb like rag dolls. Those men dressed in the black armor appeared again looking like spacemen to her, holding onto odd looking glowing weapons that were causing unbelievable mass destruction. An image of a hospital room snapped her eyes open bringing an end to the gruesome images.

The creaky door to the motel room opened slowly. As Lotus crossed the threshold Nicky followed her inside. They were both stoned out of their minds, thanks to the high grade joint they had found inside of the *New York Times* bestseller Morganna had given to Lotus. The long cross country drive had landed them in another little roach motel this time somewhere in Ohio,
"There's only one bed," Nicky whispered leaning over Lotus shoulder,
"I *know*, we only need one..." Lotus repeated turning around, "So..." her voice was low in the dark room, "Now, I got a question for you. You feeling lucky yet... *Lucky*?"

Nicky didn't answer right away instead grabbing her in his arms then with overconfidence he told her, "Always,"

"*Y'know*, there's not much difference in a gun and in a man's body...," grabbing his crotch she continued, "There's the clip...," rubbing Nicky up she added, "The barrel... and the trigger," she finished leaning in to kiss him. Nicky felt Lotus' warm wet tongue triggering his pleasure sensors and warming his loins. Her breathe was sweet and she felt like silk in his arms. They both began removing each other's clothes while continuing their passionate lip lock.

  After about an hour and a half of love making they were both naked and satisfied underneath the covers. Nicky had pleased her in a way no man had ever done before and Lotus felt a connection with him unlike anyone else in her life, it could probably have even been confused for love, "What's *wrong*?" She asked noticing Nicky's alertness.

"Still thinking about the other night," he answered truthfully.

"Well, I'm not worried about anything...," Lotus sighed snuggling up closer to him., "not *anymore*," she whispered looking up into Nicky's eyes. He kissed her then reached over to cock the hammer on the 9-mm handgun on the dresser.

Chapter 6

Three days and over 2400 miles later they found themselves finally in the hot Nevada desert only a hundred miles from their destination. The pass four days had been like a vacation for the couple. They hadn't even seen so much as a police car since they left Philadelphia International, which made Nicky wonder if this was the calm before the storm that people always talked about.

They had decided to switch vehicles yet again and this time finally had chosen one that Nicky actually approved of. The old school kitted out *Hummer* H1 sitting on black matte, *Mickey Thompson* rims was a real man's vehicle and sitting behind the wheel of the urbanized military transport he definitely felt every bit one.
"Now, this... is a *whip*...," Nicky gestured pointing a finger to the dash, "So, how much longer we got?" he asked.

Lotus had the map across the dashboard and was busy studying it intently,

"I think, about two hours... I *think*?"

Bull Dozer sat on his *Harley Davidson* watching for cars from the overpass. He and his fellow Devil Dragon brothers usually found good game on this old road. Many an innocent victim had fallen prey to one of the well-orchestrated traps set by the biker gang that turned men into sheep. There were far and few cars on the highway this time of night and when the *Hummer* came into view he picked up his walkie-talkie and squawked,
"Got a couple pigeons, black Humvee."

The music blaring inside the *Hummer* was deafening. Nicky bobbed his head to the bass heavy rock music. Looking in the rear view he saw four motorcycles relentlessly swing down besides the *Hummer*. Nicky mashed on the pedal top speed down the empty highway as two of the bikes shot out in front of them erratically,
"Now what did you do...?"
Nicky didn't reply to her. Instead he was looking in both mirrors, holding the Beretta in his right hand as he drove,
"Who'd you piss off this time?" Lotus rushed watching the motorcycles as they sped up,
"Don't worry 'bout it. Here take it," Nicky handed her the *Beretta*.
"I can't shoot that thing,"
"You can't what? Time to learn, here,"

"I'm not touching that," she was acting like she was terrified of it which didn't make since to Nicky. For a brief moment he soaked in her response then demanded that she,

"Grab on the wheel!" Nicky was leaning across her seat now aiming the *Beretta* out of the window. Lotus lunged for the steering wheel somehow managing to keep the big vehicle on the road as it swerved violently out of control. Looking through the back window Nicky aimed at the first bike he saw behind them.

A total of five bikes remained and three were directly behind them firing guns. The back window cracked as bullets burned there way inside and through the roof. Lotus screamed. Bullets were sparking holes in the roof as chips of metal and glass flew. A chopper came into Nicky's view his first shot hit the man in the side of his helmet. The bullet penetrated then exited out of the side of his face in a bloody eruption. Flipping the bike he smeared the road crimson. "Straighten it up for me!" Nicky hollered out as he lined up another shot. *'POW! hissss.'* The front tire on the lead bike popped from the gunshot and the biker atop of it lost control as his bike flipped him onto his side, spinning across the road. He was caught from behind by a second chopper that crashed into him, tossing the man on top of it to the ground like a part flying from the engine.

Nicky saw the crash then dismissed it. "Switch...," he instructed reaching into the gun bag for a fresh clip. Lotus bounced back into her seat. "Here," he gave her the clip and the *Beretta*. She watched Nicky ram the *Hummer* into one of the bikes knocking it and the man on top of it off and onto the shoulder of the road. Two more renegade bikers were still behind them like pesky vermin that were waiting for a treat to drop.

Nicky spun the wheel right taking the H1 onto a tight dirt trail that led up over and down a large hill. The bikers followed like road sharks. The Hummer began to wobble as one of the tires blew open from an echoing gunshot. Holding the wheel tightly and not letting up on his speed Nicky kept mashing, although the ride on the trail was not as smooth as before.

They were now deep off in the trail. It was getting harder for him to see so Nicky clicked the high beams on, but they were instantly drowned out when all of a sudden a brilliant high powered search light framed them like stars onstage in a Broadway musical. One of the bikers opened fire into the light hoping to hit it and was sumo slammed to the ground by a shower of 5.56-mm rounds that ate his chest for a morning snack.

"Halt return to the highway immediately or you will be shot! I repeat... you *will,* be shot!" The announcer boomed the warning twice over an outside P.A. System. The warning however came after the first biker had been shot dead. Nicky still had the radio on max and was speeding for the closed gate just in front of them slamming through the barbwire fence like a racer through the finish line. Washes of light bathed the vehicle as searchlights came on assaulting the darkness. The roof of the Humvee was punched open by more 5.56-mm bullets.
Nicky ducked low as he drove as Lotus cried out in terror flinching from the on coming bullets and sparking metal.

Bull Dozer the last man on the lone bike didn't foolishly go through the gate like his brother. Off in the distance his Harleys tail light could be seen fading away back off into the darkness.

As he surveyed his surroundings Nicky saw that they were inside of what looked like the exterior of an old prison, judging from all the watch towers located in the main yard. Whipping the big military truck into a sharp U-turn he drove back for the smashed gate. It was now or never.

Men dressed in dark fatigues ran after the *Hummer* with M4 *Carbines* held up at the ready. Nicky looked up to to see a helicopter flying overhead with a searchlight seeking the fleeing biker that had managed to escape. It looked like the gate just up ahead was clear and Nicky briefly wondered if it would actually be this easy. Nicky didn't slow down, but the *Hummer* was stopped as it violently slammed into what seemed to be thin air. Nothing was visibly in front of the gate, at least nothing that the naked eye could see. The newly updated retro-reflection projection technology utilizing *Nano-Tech* had made invisibility a reality. Those who knew of this ingenious technological discovery, also knew in the right hands it would make an unstoppable military advantage. Invisible gates were just the beginning.

Lotus slammed against the dash as the airbags knocked her windless. The seatbelt she wore also helped to save her life. Nicky's' airbag didn't go off and he felt the blunt force of the impact that left his head throbbing and spinning. The cocking of rifles all around them echoed as men in dark colored fatigues swarmed on the *Hummer*, "Driver you have approximately 10 seconds to raise your hands and step from the vehicle. Nicky turned to Lotus, "What do we do?"

Nicky turned back to look at the Black Ops soldiers, time was running out,
"We do what they say... for now," Nicky slowly crawled down from the H1 as Lotus was escorted down then around the front of the truck,
"Take them inside,"
Inside of the secret Black Ops underground base somewhere in the Nevada desert a dozen or so armed men escorted their prisoners to their superior. Several M4 *Carbines* led Nicky and Lotus down the narrow hallway at gunpoint. They came to a large freight elevator, which everyone boarded.

When the elevator came to a stop what they witnessed was a complete transformation.
The room was full of men in white lab coats at computer consoles or working furiously to solve some common problem. A squad of men were at the watch, armed with AK-105s that were up and ready.

One particular man stood out from the rest probably because of the stripes on his uniform, the sunglasses he wore in the dark room or the large *Havana* cigar he was puffing pleasurably,
"Well now, visitors," The man called T.R.I.G.G.E.R. gruffly commented.

Nicky couldn't make out the man's features clearly due mainly to the flickering glow off the monitors and flat screens located all around the room, but he looked to be clean shaven and in his early forties,

"So what's the story with you two, father disapproved of you?" The man with the sick sense of humor asked with a sinister smirk,
"What the hell is this place?" Nicky questioned looking around the room,
"*Hell*... and I am the devil..." T.R.I.G.G.E.R. answered poking a stiff thumb to his own chest,
"And upon entering my gates you are therefore my prisoners and under direction of the D.O.D. subject to execution. Anything else you need to know?" T.R.I.G.G.E.R. finished his threat sarcastically.

Nicky knew where he was, one of those government conspiracy secret military bases you only heard about through rumors or saw in movies,

"She's cute, don't tell me, you're going to Vegas to elope...?" The man with the cigar looked at the two prisoners that were ignoring his questions,
"I've got something to show you..."
This time his words caught Nicky's attention.
T.R.I.G.G.E.R. grinned, "You're gonna love this,"
As he began to signal for his men to follow him

everyone turned around as Lotus fell to the floor. Nicky ran over to her lifting her head gently in his hands, "Get back," T.R.I.G.G.E.R. shouted as one of his Black Ops commandos nudged his Carbine into Nicky's shoulder blades,

"Don't worry she'll be fine," T.R.I.G.G.E.R. assured him then ordered, "Take her to my quarters..." A big burly man in fatigues scooped up the semiconscious Lotus. Nicky grabbed for the man, but was savagely shocked by an electric stun baton. The charge made him buckle as another man joined in with a baton of his own, but somehow he kept his footing. Another powerful jolt however crumpled him and two more laid him out twitching. T.R.I.G.G.E.R. nodded to man holding Lotus as he exited the laboratory carrying her in his arms, vanishing down an adjoining corridor towards the bases resting quarters, "Five years in Afghanistan and not one man stumbles into my camp and who do I get infiltrated by, a couple of runaways,"

Nicky was dragged down the hall then dropped to the floor in a room that looked like a laser light show. The ultra-bright beams made Nicky squint as he realized why the man with the cigar wore sunglasses now,

"Look at that...," T.R.I.G.G.E.R. pointed to a weapon on a rack that looked like it had come from the future or another planet. The rifle was all chrome and had neon colored lights dancing all along its working parts. There was a long oval silencer attached to the barrel of the weapon. It was unlike any gun Nicky had ever seen or even heard about, "Pretty isn't she... she fires a sonic pulse with enough velocity to take a man's' head off his shoulders from a 1000 feet..." T.R.I.G.G.E.R. bragged, paused then continued, "Oh and in case you were wondering, you ain't going no *fucking* where..." T.R.I.G.G.E.R. picked up the futuristic sonic rifle, threw the sling over his shoulder then pointed it at Nicky, "State of the art ass kicker... we call it the *Shockwave*,"

Nicky looked at the strange looking rifle aimed at his head. It reminded him of something from the movie *Tron,* "What is this place?" he repeated.

"That's classified boy and all you need to know is you're in a whole world of shit now,"

A loud noise came from the hall something had just slammed into the door.

"Hell's going on...?" T.R.I.G.G.E.R. snarled as the men in the room aimed their M4 *Carbines* toward the sound. Another slam came right after it to give an exclamation point, "Open it up damn it,"

As the doors slide apart in falls a soldier, like a dirty bag of stinking laundry. The others take aim at the crumpled figure before immediately recognizing one of their own. Nicky sensing their confusion took action by grabbing the strange looking *Shockwave* weapon still in T.R.I.G.G.E.R.s grip, "You little bastard...," he snarled slamming a powerful stinging head butt into Nicky's face. Grunting against the pain Nicky countered with a knee to his groin, swiftly following it up with a hard head butt of his own. When Nicky's' skull crunched into T.R.I.G.G.E.R.s nose the Black Ops Commander was briefly stunned. Nicky was then able to get a firm grip squeezing on the *Shockwaves* trigger unleashing the awesome technology on the very men who had constructed it to life.

In return the unforgiving weapon vaporized one of the engineers hand as the splattered fingers made a heavy red mist in the air from the pulse rifles incredible velocity. His screams were drowned out as the weapon hummed louder with every shot, as loud as a small engine with an ear splitting high pitch. Valuable equipment was torn apart like cardboard confetti from the *Shockwave* as men ducked from the flying sparks, slivers and chunks of flying metal all over the room.

T.R.I.G.G.E.R. snapped alertness at the explosions in the room attempting to regain control of his weapon and the situation. Nicky's grip had tightened so he yanked the *Shockwave* hard enough to snap the shoulder sling, causing the gravity to pull the pulse rifle towards the ground. Both men still had firm holds on the *Shockwave* as they found themselves face to face in a showcase of superior strength, but surprisingly it was even matched. T.R.I.G.G.E.R. couldn't figure why he hadn't gained the upper hand on this little twig yet. Clearly he outweighed him by 40 to 50 pounds of muscle. The kid looked twelve to him so the wash of embarrassment that he felt was somewhat understandable.

Nicky rammed T.R.I.G.G.E.R. into one of the sparking mainframes causing a brief surge of electricity to run through the man's body. His fingers involuntarily lost some of their strength and now Nicky had control of the *Shockwave* and was now pointing it at the man who had just had him in the exact same position,

"Come on you *assholes*, *c'mon* do it, do it...!" Nicky screamed at the soldiers in the room who now had their guns aimed at his head, he knew men like them didn't miss,

"What, what, what?!" Nicky yelled.

The *Shockwave* could vaporize T.R.I.G.G.E.R.s head in microseconds and every man in there knew it. "Hold fire *goddammit*!" The direct command from their superior kept the soldiers at bay. Nicky smiled at T.R.I.G.G.E.R. who stared at the weapon pointing in his face, "Now that we've gotten all that bullshit straightened out... where is she?" Someone behind them cleared their throat loudly. Everyone turned to see Lotus standing in the doorway alone, "Miss me?" she teased wearing a sly smile.

"Take us out of here!" Nicky barked at T.R.I.G.G.E.R. lifting the *Shockwave* back up a fraction at his head,

"You haven't got the stones for it..." T.R.I.G.G.E.R. snapped glaring into the devastating device then asked, "Do you?" T.R.I.G.G.E.R. smiled at him like a snake about to strike unsuspecting prey.

Nicky returned his smile, "What makes you think she don't?" Lotus appeared at his side taking the Shockwave from Nicky. Without hesitation she let off a sonic pulse that blasted by T.R.I.G.G.E.R.. Terrified, he felt the lethal electrified air just inches away from his own face, "You crazy *bitch*!" Chuckling Nicky said, "See what I mean? Let's go... *asshole*,"

Out in the hall Nicky took the *Shockwave* from Lotus then snapped, "Close it...," T.R.I.G.G.E.R put his palm to the scanner as the door closed behind them. A blast from the *Shockwave* destroyed the scanner, "Move!" Nicky barked.

 After a few minutes of exploring the empty underground hallways Lotus impatiently asked, "Where are you taking us?"
T.R.I.G.G.E.R. ignored her as they kept walking. Stopping at an elevator he turned to them announcing, "We're here,"
"Then open it," They got on.
When the elevator finally stopped the doors opened up to reveal that they were back outside close to where all their land vehicles were parked.
"Where the fuck is our truck?" Nicky growled.
"Too bad you did what you did back there because, I was just about to show you my *real* secret weapon," T.R.I.G.G.E.R. joked unzipping his fly a little. Lotus put up her middle finger.
"Anytime," T.R.I.G.G.E.R. agreed.
Nicky pressed space-age weapon into the arrogant man's back, "You wanna try that again, where's the truck...?" T.R.I.G.G.E.R. was silent,
"Yo, *dickhead*! Don't make me turn your whole fuckin' head into red paste... I saw what this thing can do,"
 "Follow me," T.R.I.G.G.E.R. instructed knowing

that the fun was over from the burning look the boy was giving him. The Hummer was parked near the end of a line of military vehicles,

"You drive it," Nicky told Lotus who reached for the driver door when a gunshot rang out from one of the guards standing in the tower hitting the back door of the Hummer.

"*Shit*," T.R.I.G.G.E.R. cursed pulling a high tech plastic covert knife from his shin sheath reaching for the Oriental girl climbing behind the wheel of the Hummer. Nicky turned his attention from T.R.I.G.G.E.R. to the man shooting at them from above. He squeezed the trigger and the *Shockwave* buckled the tower supports dropping the guy to the ground bouncing and broken from the impact. Turning back he saw that T.R.I.G.G.E.R. held the plastic knife poised to strike at Lotus,

"No!" The *Shockwave* briefly went off as T.R.I.G.G.E.R.s' hand and the plastic blade splattered into red mist and tiny shiny black bits. The Black Ops leaders screams of pain were almost as loud as the *Hummers* engine. Lotus had finally cranked the ignition,

"Can we go?!" she rushed.

Nicky looked back towards the commotion he heard coming from behind the facility.

More armed men exited the base firing assault rifles at them. Nicky slammed Lotus' door then bolted around the vehicle leaving T.R.I.G.G.E.R. writhing and bleeding out in the dirt. When he got around the side of the *Hummer* Nicky returned fire with the *Shockwave*.

Four of the twelve or so men shooting rifles at them were hit by the electrified air. Most lost limbs and one unfortunate man lost half of his face as the entire side of his skull was turned into blood and bone spray from the *Shockwaves* velocity. Despite the loss of personnel or seeing their commanding officer squirming in the dirt in complete agony they continued shooting at Nicky. "The *ice*...?" Nicky jumped in slamming his door, "Did they get it?!" Lotus shook her head, "They're still under the dash," she assured him as she spun the powerful *Hummer* speeding it directly at the trigger happy commandos shooting at them. One round hit one of the rear tires as it passed crushing two of the mercs under its huge frame crunching them over.

The vehicle bounced then wobbled a bit as Lotus struggled to hold the wheel steady, "Now what?" she asked,
"Go left.!"
"Where am I going?" Lotus looked to Nicky for the answer.

"Head for the chopper,"

"A *motorcycle*?"

"No... the helicopter,"

"Do you know how to fly?"

Lotus was wild eyed when Nicky shot back,

"Nope, you?"

Aleksandr Kazachansky sat inside the helicopter listening to his Mp3 player headset. The rap music blaring from it was in Russian and he nodded rhythmically to the song as the *Hummer* pulled up parking near the helipad.

Aleksandr removed his earplugs when he saw a teenage American boy and an Asian girl run up to him pointing their American allies new age weapon directly at him. From instinct he raised his arms as Nicky asked,

"*S'up*, we was on our way to the *Strip* to get married... you don't mind giving up a lift, do you?"

"*Da*... yes, do not shoot,"

Mr. H.A.M.M.E.R. was officially the second officer in command of base operations and was the one who ordered the men to fire at the escaping prisoners. So deep down he felt the loss of his superior's left hand could partially been his doing.

Fortunately for him however what most men would call their guilty conscience wasn't a part of his genetic code, "*Hell,*" he thought aloud as the gurney rolled up carrying a morphined T.R.I.G.G.E.R. He knew he had done a lot worst to women and children, "How we feeling?" Mr. H.A.M.M.E.R. asked expressionlessly.

"Who gave that order to fire upon the civilians?" T.R.I.G.G.E.R. asked him clearly under the influence of the morphine,

"The D.O.D. gave the order, you know that… that any and all who find out…"

"You son of a *bitch!*" T.R.I.G.G.E.R. yelled as he began reaching for a sidearm from one of the commandos pushing his stretcher. The *Beretta* 92F came easily from the holster and was now pointed at H.A.M.M.E.R's head, "You put the life of your commanding officer in endangerment mister, therefore committing an act of treason on US soil…"

"Are you *insane*? You know just as well as I that," The bullet that pierced Mr. H.A.M.M.E.R's brain answered his question with an all too deadly yes, "And I still got one good hand…," T.R.I.G.G.E.R. spat sneering down at H.A.M.M.E.R.'s corpse.

"Gentlemen, Operation Shock Therapy has now been compromised. Find me the boy, the girl, my missing weapon and get me some mores drugs!"

The Las Vegas skyline was absolutely beautiful as the sun rose from the east, the helicopter flew west, "Look at that..." Lotus pointed back toward the rising sun snuggling up closer to Nicky whispering, "don't you think we should really do it?"

"Do what?"

"You *know*," she said looking into his eyes with a dreamy look that locked him in.

"*Um*... just land us over there," Nicky told the pilot who nodded his head in agreement.

Hovering over of the building Nicky had picked the pilot eased the throttle lowering the aircraft down to the roof of what looked like an office building. The helicopter touched down as the blades whirled sending dust flying over the sides. Aleksandr turned to Nicky for instructions, "Okay, now get out of here...," Nicky ordered, then told Lotus, "C'mon, let's go... *Hey*, what the hell is you doing?!"

The pilot had caught his attention reaching under the dash to hit the homing beacon for his comrades to find his position, had he waited a few more seconds he might have been much more successful, but that was only half of his mission.

The *Stechkin* 9-mm machine-pistol he came back with didn't surprise Nicky, but what happened next did. The machine-pistol went off as fast as it had appeared missing his face by inches. The shot rang out in the cockpit like an explosion followed by a blast from the *Shockwave,* which let off its deadly pulse as the Russian pilots head exploding it in a haze of blood, bone and brain matter. Nicky snatched Lotus from the back seat as they ran from the helipad. Nicky blasted the lock off of the door that lead inside dropping the *Shockwave* right there on the roof as they both ran down the steps.

Chapter 7

Nicky sat on the plush waterbed inside the expensive four star hotel located a few miles from the *Strip*. This was a major upgrade from their last place. Three hours had passed since that fateful encounter out in the desert had occurred. Nicky was now busy looking through the new bag of guns that he had just stolen. Some of every kind was inside there at least 12 of them with a few boxes of ammo too. For a brief moment Nicky felt nostalgic at the sight of all those firearms and almost longed to be back behind the counter at his grandfather's gun shop back in Queens.

Lotus stood by the window turning to stare at Nicky in disbelief. She had been looking at him like that off and on ever since he had decided to rob the one eyed pimp in charge of the strip club she once worked at a long time ago, but that was another story. The pimp who ran *'Candyland'* had a notorious temper and being robbed by an ex-dancers supposed husband was only going to boil it over. And now thanks to *Lucky*, they now had another group of guns coming after them, again.

"Nice..." Nicky zipped the bag close,
"Now, what about something to eat?" Nicky
asked conversationally,
"I can't believe you did that."
Nicky shrugged at Lotus,
"What can I say, you inspired me with that gas
station you robbed back in *Jersey*,"
"You know, this pissing people of thing of yours?"
"Yeah, what about it?" his tone was defensive.
Lotus looked him square in the eye, held his
serious gaze for a breath or two then admitted,
"You real good at it,"
Nicky was speechless, he didn't know if it was a
compliment or criticism. The booming drums
coming from the ceiling broke the silence,
"*Damn*, what the hell is this a hotel or the studio?"
Nicky got up heading for the door stuffing the
newly acquired gold *Desert Eagle* into his
waistband then covering it up with his shirt.
  Lotus sighed loudly, "Now what are you going
to do?" she was sitting on the waterbed watching
as Nicky cracked the hotel door peering out of it,
"I'm a just go check things out, don't open up this
door for anybody but me," he explained,
"Don't you think you pissed enough people off for
one night?"
Nicky didn't respond to that. Stepping silently out
of the room he locked the hotel door behind him.

On the top floor of the four star hotel in the penthouse suite an up and coming rock band was busy rocking the entire building and not to mention trashing the room, after all it was Rock & Roll tradition. The heavy metal quartet occupied the room with three of their voluptuous tattooed groupies that had left the mosh pit with them and rode back in the rented stretch *Bentley* limousine.

Once the girls saw it pull up they were as good as screwed. After a steamy all night orgy that had lasted well into the morning hours, two of the girls were now passed out in one of the beds together.

Most of his life Melvin Chesterfield had always been considered kind of weird or bizarre. All during his tormented childhood up into his wild teens, finally finding his groove one night at his senior high school talent show, where he stepped onstage and into the future. Dressed in a metal hauberk, skin tight tiger print pants and clear stilettos, the mouths dropped and the heads began nodding as he commenced tearing the house down. Looking back he considered that officially the night the *rock superstar* 'SEX-Z' was born.

Still rocking to the pounding drums he jumped down from one of the beds quickly moving across the room like an animated bird swooping down to the table for a nose dive into a small miniature mountain of high grade pure Colombian cocaine.

"Woooo...!" he shouted victoriously coming up with his nose covered in the white powder, "*Hey...* go get Larry on the line and tell him to get us some more of nose candy over here!" he was yelling at his lead guitar player, 'Freak E' who was so stoned out of his mind he could barely pay attention. He was too busy watching one of the girls dancing naked to the banging drums. A loud knock on the door broke his gaze, "What the hell is this...?!" Sex-Z asked getting even more hyper. Sprinting over to the door, snatching it open he yelled, "Who in the hell are you... the *fuckin'* bell boy?"

Nicky stood in the doorway staring back at the odd looking dude. The tall guy was shirtless and looked like skin and bones. He had milky white skin that looked like it had been bleached and oily jet black hair that hung pass his shoulder. His face was painted with deep dark mascara around his eyes kind like a baseball player looking into the sun. To Nicky he looked like a skinny vampire, "What... *nah,* look me and my wife just got married, okay and we're on our honeymoon. So we were just hoping that you guys could keep it down a little, that's all," Nicky told him. "Down?" Sex-Z questioned sounding offended, "Yeah... if it's not too much trouble," Sex-Z looked out into the hallway asking,

"Where's Spike, Butchie?"

Nicky shrugged,

"Look, I got to get back to my wife, but I would really appreciate you guys lowering the music just a little bit..." A waiter coming up the hallway caught his attention stopping his motion,

"Yo, you order some food?" Nicky turned to Sex-Z who blurted,

"Hey who's got the munchies?"

At that moment Spike and Butch, the bands personal security team came walking down the hall from the opposite direction of the waiter.

"Hey, *Boss*... everything okay?" Spike asked.

"Where the hell you two cocksuckers been, huh?" They both walked up eyeballing Nicky,

"Sorry, Boss, coffee break. It won't happen again,"

"It better not, you two stay right here, Larry's on his way up so..."

The waiter who was hanging around by one of the other rooms down the hall subtly removed a silenced MP5SD from underneath the cart he was wheeling. Nicky spotted the action immediately,

"*Shit*, gun!" Pushing Sex-Z into the penthouse Nicky whipped out the *Desert Eagle*, cocking the large weapon,

"Fuckin' A!" Sex-Z exclaimed staring at the hand cannon in awe.

The man with the silenced MP5SD fired rapidly at Spike and Butch who were both caught like ducks in a shooting gallery.

Trying to evade was useless and when the first rounds impacted them in the face, neck and chest firing back was as well. Spike collapsed into the wall head first and Butch crumpled over him. Both men were left gushing crimson from the face and tubular cavities. The waiter ignored their suffering swinging his weapon inside the penthouse. The gunfire had stirred a flutter from the other band members who all depended on Spike and Butch for their very safety. Nicky and Sex-Z ran into the room avoiding five whispering silenced shots. "What the *fuck*, bro?!" yelled 'Nast-D' the band's drummer who had been at the bar still doing lines. With no time to answer or stop moving Nicky simply ran in diving behind the bed that was next to the giant glass window overlooking fabulous sin city below. 'Horn-E' the bands keyboard player and part time roadie, slammed the door shut as ran to crouch down behind one of the tables.

The bed was so big that Nicky couldn't even see the two girls that had already been hiding until he actually hit the floor landing in a heap next to the terrified half-naked groupies. Sex-Z was sluggish from all the drinking & drugs, before he even reached the bed the door to the penthouse flew back open. Nicky quickly put a bullet into the doorknob causing the door to fly back into the man groin as he entered doubling him over onto the penthouse floor. Reaching for his balls with his free hand still trying to aim the SMG at someone he spit two shots hitting Nast-D dead in his chest as blood spray soaked the white powder still on top of the bar,

"Aaaaaaaaah!"

The groupie girls screamed as three more men wearing hotel security uniforms and sunglasses entered the room carrying more of those silenced MP5SDs. Nicky finished the waiter off with a.44 Magnum to the brain then ducked back behind the bed frame. The security guards opened up with their silenced SMGs as the final two band members were cut to pieces from their endless onslaught that continued to chew the room apart.

The king size they hid behind had been stacked so high with mattresses that the sheets barely hung down over the sides giving Nicky an excellent view underneath of his would be executioners legs. The *Desert Eagle* held 8 rounds and Nicky wanted to make every one of them count. He fired a single shot hitting the him low grossly shattering his anklebone. The severe pain bent the man over dropping him to the ground.

Through the brief moment of eye contact the men shared the man's pain was apparent, so Nicky decided to do him a favor. Brains and bone exploded all over his brothers in arms shoes as they began concentrating their remaining firepower on the bed tearing it to shreds. When one he heard their SMGs clack empty, Nicky recognized the sound all too well. Without any hesitation he lifted himself up, firing the *Desert Eagle* rapidly. The first round hit the clip he was holding as one guard attempting to reload his weapon. Dropping the magazine from what was left of his now bleeding hand, Nicky turned the guys sub-machine gun into a useless piece of metal. 'BOOM' In and out, the slug from the *Desert Eagle* caught it dead in the face. The last guy was reaching for his fallen companions sub machine gun when two shots burned their way through his pelvis bone. The guy stumbled over the corpse laying next to him landing on his back in complete torment. Before the guy could focus his eyes Nicky had the silenced MP5SD he was reaching for, aiming both weapons dead in his face,
"Who sent you?"
The man grimaced a hard smile, but remained silent, "What... is... his... name?" each word came with a nudge from the big pistol. The man's menacing expression stayed locked on his face as

he held Nicky's intense gaze.

Sex-Z was now kneeling, holding the now deceased Nast-D by the hand, sobbing loudly while the two remaining girls rubbed his shoulders. Nicky realized that the four of them were all lucky to live through this deadly experience. He also knew these guys were from that lab out in the desert and that they were pros and pros didn't send in all their hitters at once. More men were coming., "Yo, everybody out now!" Nicky yelled.

The girls who snapped to attention from the urgency in his voice both grabbed two long T-shirts off of the bed. Frantically running into the hallway still half-naked the girls didn't look back. Sex-Z looked up at Nicky with glassy eyes then asked him, "You know who did this don't you?" Nicky shook his head slowly then pointed at the man he had left alive, "He does,"

Storming over to the fallen man Sex-Z picks up the silenced MP5SD the first guy dropped aiming it at his head, "Who did this…? I said who you son of a *bitch*!"

"Don't do it man, piece of *shit* ain't worth it..." Nicky's words fell deaf to the rock stars unflinching determination to kill this man.

"You got too much to live for..." Nicky breathed lowering the gun in Sex-Z hands.

After taking a deep breath then letting it out the enraged musician finally listened to the kid,

"You okay?" Nicky asked quietly,

"Yeah... I'm good,"

"Good, come on,"

"What about this, prick?" Sex-Z asked.

"Leave him, he's got a lot of explaining to do,"

Out in the hallway Nicky looked for more gun toting guards, but saw no one. He did however notice that all the video cameras in the hall had been destroyed. When they got down the hall towards the end they heard a grunt coming from behind. Spinning they saw that it was the man Nicky had shot in the ass, the one he had just stopped the Rocker from killing two seconds ago. "Watch it!" Nicky hollered as Sex-Z pulled a move from one of his music videos minus the prop guns. He turned and fired the silenced SMG in one motion that would have made 007 himself jealous. The man caught the 9-mm Parabellum in the head and dropped his freshly loaded MP5SD.

After a brief moment of silence Nicky admitted, "Good shot..." picking up the SMG, checking the clip, then taking and extra magazine off the dead man's body, "Come on."

When Nicky first left the room Lotus was still a little mad at him, but it quickly passed. She became more and more troubled about being alone and found herself aiming the jeweled *Derringer* at the door. The pink diamond handle glistened in her tiny fist.

After five minutes of staring at the chain lock she sighed then put the platinum pistol back inside of the *attaché* case. She did decide however to take Nicky's gym bag collection of guns into the bathroom with her as she jumped in the shower.

The stinging water relaxed her from head to toe, running through her black silky hair all down her nude frame. She stopped the water when the phone rang. Rushing from the bathroom still wet, wearing only a towel on her head she answered it quickly, "Yes?"

The voice on the line was deep and confident. "Yes, ma'am there's been a disturbance in the building and we've been instructed by authorities to evacuate the hotel one floor at a time. You are advised to remain in your room, ma'am until security arrives to escort you safely from the building,"

"What's happening?" Lotus questioned the man unsure of what to do next,

"We'll be there shortly to explain everything to you, ma'am." then the line went dead.

Lotus turned to the door confused. When Nicky had gotten into that gun fight a few floors up, she had been taking a shower and was unable to hear clearly. She had thought that maybe the building was under construction was probably being worked on or something. So the mysterious phone call from the front desk came as a surprise to her. Then she remembered who it was she was with, "That was fast," she said to herself thinking out loud. She was referring to Nicky and his ability at pissing off complete strangers.

She had just finished putting her clothes on when the expected door knock finally came. Although she knew it was coming she still jumped at the sound. Inching from the bed to the door she hesitated for a moment before asking,

"What is this all about?" Looking through the peephole she saw two man standing at her hotel door dressed in security uniforms,

"There's a gunman in the hotel, we're evacuating everyone I need you to open this door ma'am,"

"My husband... he's still in the hotel. I have to find him first,"

"Don't worry ma'am I'm sure he's safe, now the door, please," The smaller guard ordered as he attempted to turn the handle. When Lotus saw this she slowly backed away from the door a little, inching her way backwards towards the waterbed.

Nicky and Sex-Z sprinted down the staircase, making their way for the door to the seventh floor. "Look just stay back, let me do the shooting, *alright?*"

"You got it, bro,"

Nicky snatched it open aiming the silenced SMG down the empty hall, "Come on."

When they turned down the hall that led to his room they saw two big dudes wearing those same fake security guard uniforms that the corpses upstairs in Sex-Z's room were wearing trying to get into his hotel room,

"Yo, *dickhead*?!"

When the mercenaries turned around Nicky greeted the one on the left with two hot shots, one hitting his forehead and the other landing just under his left eye. He spun then fell instantly as his partner attempted to line up the barrel of his own pistol with Nicky's head. The hotel door opened as Lotus ran out chopping the guy gun from his hand, sending it sliding down the carpeted hallway. Nicky's next three shots caught him deep in his torso punching him into the wall leaving only a crumpled corpse,

"Well, what the hell are you waiting for...?"

Nicky yelled at Lotus who hesitated for a heartbeat, "Get over here already!"

She quickly ran up to them looking Sex-Z over with a hard eye, "Who's this?"

"Grab our shit, we're leaving," Nicky demanded. "Now where are we go?"

"Babe...!" he interrupted, "Dead bodies, can we go... *please*?"

Giving Nicky a quick peck on the cheek she replied, "*Un huh*, but only because you asked me so nicely..." before she ran back into the room.

A few seconds later she came back with the small *attaché* case and the gym bag full of guns,

"Here, make yourself some use," Lotus insisted handing the gym bag over to Sex-Z,

"*Whaaat*?! Who you think I am, the roadie or something? In case you were wondering you are now looking at thee most bad ass... this side of Sunset. The one, the only, the *living legend!*" Thrusting his pelvis forward as he spoke he gyrated his hips to emphasize his point to her, "Rock superstar of the century... Sex-Z Z Z Z... Z!"

"Whatever..." Lotus muttered rolling her eyes unimpressed, "here,"

When they finally made it to the lobby there was a lot of activity down there as LVPD squad cars were just now pulling into the hotels parking lot.

"Come on, tour bus is this way," Sex-Z insisted.

Lotus followed Nicky and the rock-n-roll Goth out of one of the side doors into the parking lot towards the direction of a large tour coach that had Sex-Z's white painted face with his trademark black mascara around his eyelids on the side of it, "Damn it!" Sex-Z stopped at the door of his bus. "What is it?" Nicky asked, "They killed Spike...!" The rocker shouted then dug into his pants pockets removing a set of large keys, "Can any one of you, crazy kids drive?" Lotus snatched the keys from his hand then shot Nicky a sexy mischievous grin.

Mr. T.R.I.G.G.E.R. sat inside the infirmary at the underground base located somewhere out in the Nevada desert when he saw that he had a surprise visitor. The tall Russian man with the hard face, cold eyes and blonde buzz cut walked up to him flanked by two equally menacing looking brutes, "Comrade, I am most glad you have only lost a hand and not your life," The man called Mr. A.K. commented in a heavy accent. The words were an attempt at showing some concern for their American allies well being, but the emotionless tone let the truth be known, he didn't give a damn if the man's balls had been blown off into a million pieces, so long as their joint mission was a success.

What had brought him to the man was the news that his younger brother who had come over with him from Moscow to be his personal pilot was now a hostage of the American man and Asian woman, at the moment that was his only concern. He was confident in his brothers military training that he would be able to handle the American boy. The fact that the man he now stood over who stared up at him with a look in his eyes Mr. A.K. could only describe as weakness, had no type of information on their whereabouts left him feeling only disgust., '*Americans*...?' he thought, 'nothing but a*ll talk*,'

The groan T.R.I.G.G.E.R. made broke into A.K.s thoughts, "Gentlemen..." Another grunt followed, "Operation 'Shock Therapy' has *not* been compromised. I assure you that the man and woman will be found within 24 hours, I guarantee this,"

"And what of Aleksandr?"

"My men are checking for them on the satellites, we'll have them shortly,"

"I hope for your sake, comrade... you do that,"

Mr. A.K.s flat tone left a sinister air in the room that Mr. T.R.I.G.G.E.R. tried to chuckle off,

"Is that a threat, mister?"

"I do not make threats, I only give warnings and let us not forget that our relationship is not outside

of our common mission and make no mistake if I
have to... I will," Mr. A.K. turned and walked
from the bed leaving the man called T.R.I.G.G.E.R.
pondering his words.

 Lotus drove the tour bus into downtown Las
Vegas sometime around 4 pm. And was having
the time of her life as she spun the big wheel,
bouncing in the large seat as Sexpression's music
boomed from the speakers like cannon fire.
Nicky was a little surprised that some of it actually
sounded good to him. The song playing was
called *Like a Suicidal Vampire* Sex- Z was busy
banging his head to the guitar riffs when he
stopped and blurted, "Here... we're here, put us
over there!" Sex-Z pointed to a store with a large
stuffed alligator in the window,
"Put it over there, *Sweet Stuff*..."
Lotus whipped the big bus into the parking lot
with the precision of cutting glass, then slammed
it into park at the spot Sex-Z had pointed out to
her. Turning to Nicky she beamed so bright at him
that he had to blink, "Okay first things first.
Now I understand you two got the whole bad ass
with a gun thing going on and you with the
gangster geisha girl vibe, but... If we're going to
kick some ass the right way, we got to look good
first!"

"What's wrong with the way we look?" Nicky asked sounding a little offended,

"Nothing, like I said I'm feeling you guys, it's just now you guys are with a fashion guru, so I'm giving you two a well needed *upgrade*,"

The Strap was a popular store near the Strip to lots of entertainers in the city and the man named Cowboy who ran the place wasn't at all surprised when Sex-Z himself walked in. He had seen one of his live shows over at the 'The Nut House' a popular burlesque joint and really dug the S&M that was taking place on stage.

"Oh my goodness, I don't F-ing believe it. I am such.... a huge fan of yours. Would you be needing something for one of your shows perhaps... loved you at The Nut House by the way. So what will it be?"

Sex-Z whips a .44 magnum *Colt Anaconda* out,

"Yeah, here's the thing... we're going to need you to lock all the doors and give us some private service,"

"That's a big gun..." Cowboy blurted,

Sex-Z loudly cocks back the hammer suggesting that Cowboy get to it, "Right away, Mr. Sex-Z, sir... Mads, Kenney get the doors, now!"

Two young ladies, Madison and Kennedy came from behind the counter and quickly locked the front doors rushing back over to their manager who was still held at gunpoint.

"Okay do something with these two, I'm thinking leather and gator,"

"We'll take care of them, sir... girls!"

Cowboy clapped his hands as the girls escorted Nicky and Lotus over to the dressing rooms.

After coming out and trying on about three different wardrobes, Sex-Z finally agreed upon a skin tight red & black open back dress for Lotus, that had a white flower stitched across the front of it to match the pink one tattooed on her back. She also had a little pink purse where she put the platinum *Derringer* along with the diamonds, dumping the attaché case in the garbage,

"Didn't I tell you I was a fuckin' genius or what... and you?" The rocker bragged referring to the burgundy Alligator skin pants, black silk shirt, *Gucci* frames and shoes Nicky was now wearing,

"Now you look *lucky*, how you two feeling...?" Sex-Z asked excitedly loving their new look,

"You guys ready to rock?"

Nicky and Lotus gave each other a quick head to toe then Lotus answered,

"Rock... and *roll*,"

"*Yeaaah!*" Sex-Z boomed then yelled,

"Alright, now let's go kick this cities ass!"

CASINO TRIPLE 7 LAS VEGAS STRIP

The newly constructed cash house was close to the high end luxury Casinos located further down the Strip, but had not yet received the clientele of say a *Caesars Palace* or *MGM*. That was however quickly changing as more and more celebrities began to frequent the game house.

When Nicky, Lotus, Sex-Z, Cowboy, Madison and Kennedy walked inside the *Casino Triple 7* the commotion of people, music and bells going off hit them in the face like a jab from the Greatest himself.

"The King is in the *fuckin'* building..!" Sex-Z shouted as people stopped and turned to see what was going on, "I... am... *home!* Come on boys and girls..." Sex-Z shoved Cowboy out front of him then wrapped his arms around the two girls guiding them all off towards the gaming tables. He turned to look back at Nicky and Lotus, "Look you two, I'm starting to feel lucky my damn self. So you go find these jerks while I take my new good luck charms here and go win us some honey, *money... money money!*"

Lotus watched the four of them disappear somewhere into the slots then turned to Nicky saying, "I thought they'd never leave,"

"Let's go and play a few games before we go upstairs, see if we see anything funny first,"

"Whatever you say, *koibito*,"

"What's that mean?"

"Lover,"

Nicky looked in her face and saw that loving expression in her eyes again then leaned over to kiss her cheek saying, "Let's go get lucky,"

Lotus put her arm in the crook of Nicky's elbow walking close to him through the ringing slot machines, "I can't believe we're finally here..." Nicky didn't say anything. Lotus looked to him the hard expression on his face reminding her of the deadly situation they were both still very much apart of, "How 'bout this?" Lotus asked pointing to the craps table. It was nice and packed with gamblers. She had spotted an opening just big enough for the two of them so they squeezed in next to an old timer who greeted them with a genuine smile and a friendly nod, "Howdy,"

Time was flying, probably because they were actually starting to have fun. Nicky threw the dice and was now on his third pass, racking up chips for himself and the other players who happened to not be betting against the kid in the expensive sunglasses, who looked like a mini mobster in training. His next toss landed on 4 and the old guy next to him reached over to pick up a stack of black chips sliding one over to Nicky, "Good job,"

"Do it again,"

"I told you this was fate," Lotus' husky whisper vibrated in Nicky's ear. as he shook the dice then released them,

"Yo, another winner... winner yo," the dealer announced as the table loudly cheered Nicky on. This time it was an 11 and it seemed Nicky was finally living up to his nick-name when everything was shot to hell. At that exact moment Nicky was picking up the chips he had just won, Big Gus Falcone, the same guy he had shot in the foot in the motel parking lot back in *Jersey* a few days ago was now carrying a tray with a cheeseburger and a glass of diet Coca-Cola on it, staring right at him, "I'll be damn, *heeere*... the little bastards over here...!" Gus shouted at the top of his heavy lungs, "*Heeeere!*"

Carmine Giordano looked up when he heard Gus' voice. Three of his goons ran to his aid, when they caught up to Carmine he was pointing them in the direction of the craps tables. He was a little surprised to find them so soon. He knew they were in town from one of his marks at the hotel where the gunfight Nicky had gotten into took place, but he didn't expect to find them this early. Carmine was the Underboss of Las Vegas for the family and when Donnie called and told them to expect the kid and the girl a few days ago, he put word out all around town to be on the lookout.

Nicky took off snatching Lotus' by the wrist like he did the first time they had met back in his grandfather's gun store, it was starting to become routine. They pushed their way through the crowds of losers and small time winners fleeing the fat gangster. Nicky's first mind told him to get out of the building, that it had all been a set up since the motel. Security were now swarming the area, but Nicky and Lotus managed to slip through unnoticed by the dozen or so armed guards rushing pass them.

 "Fuck, they're getting away!" Gus warned, "Oh no they ain't," Carmine responded by reaching under his jacket for his 9-mm GLOCK, "Wait..." Gus laid an arm across Carmines shoulder. The big man was getting winded and didn't feel up for a gunfight with the LVPD.

 Nicky and Lotus made it far as the fourth step that led up to the Casino exit when the doors were blasted apart sending flying chunks glass pass them. Nicky and Lotus ducked from a concussive force that came from the now opened exit. Nicky and Lotus ran back behind a row of slot machines as more shrapnel made of glass and brass showered all around them. Everyone in the Casino turned towards the doors to witness the horrific site as twelve men wearing black armor that shined like it had been made from black diamonds appeared in the obliterated entrance. A brief silence followed then a lone voice cried out, "What the hell's going on?!"

The armored headgear the men wore brought forth images of the famous movie space villain Darth Vader. Their tinted visors on the front of their helmets made it look like a mini gas mask, but without the hose fixtures around the mouth area, mixed with a dirt bike helmet adding to its futuristic menacing look. One thing was for certain these guys were not a part of the nightly entertainment.

The men in the black armor were called Shocktroopers and they were the ground force of Operation: 'Shock Therapy' which was intended to introduce a new breed of terrorism to the world. The devastating weapons they carried were about to be advertised across the world on CNN in what was going to be the biggest, deadliest fundraiser in American history.

Once the world's foremost terrorist states saw the Armageddon like power of these weapons and the potential of mass destruction they offered when constructed on a larger scale, then that's when the cash registers would start and would never stop ringing all across the globe.

Although this joint venture with ex-Russian *Spetsnaz* commandos and Military Intelligence had extraordinary rewards there were risk due to exposure, but on the other hand it fell mainly on the Russians who now wore the black armor.

It was true that if they were caught and questioned they all had more than enough knowledge to incriminate some high ranking individuals in the US Government, if so then a few well planned prison executions was just a phone call away. Besides from the Russians point of view the weapon itself was so unstoppable that if anything or anyone was stupid enough to get in their way, they would instantly be torn to bloody bits. The lead Shocktroop fired upon the slot machines where Nicky and Lotus were still hiding. A sonic boom blasted the machine in half.

Big Gus, Carmine and his three Mafia soldiers rushed up firing straight at the robot looking bozos at the door, "Where's the kid?" Gus yelled firing nonstop at them. The dozen or so rounds the gangsters put into them didn't do any damage to their armor. This time the lead Shocktrooper turned his sights on the out of shape wimps in the suits firing peashooters at him and his men. The man he caught with the electrified beam lost his gun along with his whole arm at the shoulder.

It was sent flying like a spinning baton that landed on top of some guys head knocking the man to the floor.

Gus ducked off to the side when he saw Mario's arm take flight trailing after the kid from the gun store. He limped after them fuming at the thought of getting some payback on the little punk for what he did to him. After they got the jewels back he planned on shooting a few of his toes off, if he could just catch the little, "*Shit,*"

Nicky and Lotus ran out of the main Casino floor entering into the hotel lobby. Nicky was still holding the gun and one of the two security guards standing near the front desk noticed quickly reaching for his holstered revolver which Nicky accurately shot off of his hip. The other guard was drawing his weapon when Nicky shot the gun from his hand before he could raise it. Too stunned to properly react all they could do was raise their arms up high in surrender, "How do you do that?" Lotus was baffled as Nicky's remarkable shooting ability as she stared at the two guards dumbfounded,

Nicky grabbed her by her wrist again. After kicking the guards guns far out of their reach, they both ran for the steps. When they got to the staircase they heard, "Hey, kid...!"

They stopped then turned to see Big Gus Falcone breathing heavy and brandishing a SIG-*Sauer* P220, "I just want to cut a deal, just between me and you," They responded by turning and running up the stairs., "*Shit*...!" Gus shouted as he limped pass the guards growling, "*Fuck* out of the way...," he fired a shot from the bottom of the stairs that went high above Nicky's head as the two of them entered the door to the second floor. "Damnit!" Gus' face reflected exactly how he was feeling. His foot was killing him, the kid was becoming a real pain in the ass and he was still hungry. He limped for the elevator, he knew what floor the real party was on.

The second floor was empty despite the fact World War III was going on downstairs in the *Casino Triple 7*. No complaints here Nicky thought as they ran around the corner bumping into a hotel maid and her cleaning cart knocking it over, "Sorry 'bout that," Nicky was helping the young lady up with his free hand. Seeing the *Beretta* she gasped frantically running in the opposite direction in complete terror.
"No, wait, wait...."
"Come, on!" this time Lotus yanked him by the arm. They made it to the next stairwell then quickly proceeded up to the seventh floor.

Making it there without any difficulties Nicky cracked the seventh floor door peeking into the hall. Unlike downstairs there was absolute pure panic going on up here. People ran for the elevators where a large crowd had formed around them. Virtually the entire floor was trying to leave all at once.

"Now...!" Nicky and Lotus ran into the throng making their way towards room 777. The halls were narrow so getting through was a bit challenging, "Should be just around the corner," Nicky reassured her. The crowd was starting to thin out a bit and as it did a familiar image took shape causing Nicky to pause,

"*What*, what is it?" Lotus asked as they saw the fat gangster limping through the crowd. Nicky took aim, "Okay, big boy. If that's how you want... round two,"

Expertly shooting through the fleeing people he sent another bullet straight into Big Gus' already damaged foot. The loud explosion from the pistol made everyone in the hall crouch all but Gus who collapsed from the bullets impact. He was already in tremendous pain, but now he was in agony. He fired his entire clip down the hall hitting two innocent bystanders in the thigh and lower back.

Nicky and Lotus finally made it to room 777 the door was wide open. Nicky aimed the *Beretta* through the door, "Stay behind me..."

Lotus fastened herself to his back, "No... I want you to stay out here," she nodded as he entered scanning the room carefully. Searching the bathroom Nicky discovered that a corpse was in there, some young Hispanic guy. Someone had shot him in the head then stuffed him face down in the bathtub, like he had just committed suicide, twice. Nicky decided he had seen enough,

"Nothing," Nicky lied to her stepping back out closing the door behind him. Pulling Lotus back down the hall toward the hysterical hotel guest he heard,

"Hey, kid?!"

Nicky turned aiming the gun to see some older looking white guy with beady hard eyes wearing a cheap suit staring back at him. The guy looked more like a cop rather than a gangster to Nicky. Again he felt like this was all one big set up, "Show me *yo* badge, bitch!" Nicky demanded pointing the *Beretta,*

"What...?" Benedict snapped offended, then asked. "Who the *hell* are you anyway, I thought Koji was coming to make the exchange?" Benedict added the question looking to Lotus who blinked, then froze at the mention of the name of the man she

103

had poisoned a few days ago. Benedict slightly smirked at her display of what he considered a common reaction of guilt,

"You got the *merch* or what?" he asked coolly. Nicky's' head twitched almost as if some sixth sense of his was warning him to look pass the whiny man. Down near the end of the hall were two of those guys dressed in the black armor that had just shot the Casino floor up with those space-age weapons from the underground base out there in the desert. It looked like the two of them now had there sights on the two of them.

"You listening to me or... what the?" Benedict turned his head in the direction Nicky was looking were he saw the armored killers coming for them

It seemed that the lead Shocktroop had decided to take a personal vendetta against Nicky from the Casinos entrance. Since then he had blasted a path of destruction directly towards him. Now he was at the end of the hall and all that stood in his way were a few American vermin.'No problem,' he thought because he had the perfect extermination device.

The technology that created the *Shockwaves* had been designed to destroy large asteroids in outer space, but like many military inventions its use in war or in this case terrorism was inevitable.

The weapon hummed and sent forth a hot electrified beam that tore chunks from about four fleeing people. A large hole was punched into one of the walls and into the adjoining rooms. Turning his *Shockwave* in the young man's direction the lead Shocktroop unleashed more devastation volley,

Benedict hadn't seen the power of the *Shockwaves* downstairs, he had been too busy upstairs on the 7th floor cleaning up the blood spray and stuffing another corpse into the bathtub. He thought the guys might have been some form of L.V.P.D. S.W.A.T, but when he saw them rip innocent bystanders into human flesh puzzles he decided he had better take cover too. Hours on the gun range paid off for him in one or two firefights. The Detective's first shot hit the lead Shocktroop square in the visor. His head popped back leaving his weapon hanging limply at his side hooked to a shoulder sling. The man next to him let his weapon hum as the very corner Benedict had been hiding behind exploded dropping him to the floor on his backside, after catching a face full of drywall.

The lead Shocktroop raised back up. His visor appeared to have a small chip in it from the gunshot, but there were no more signs of further damage. The armor they wore was truly amazing.

He raised his weapon once more as if he were just stung by a bee. Through the flying red mist he and his comrade had showered the 7th floor with he saw Nicky and Lotus running into one of the rooms down the hall. The Shocktroopers swarmed into the room releasing a wall smashing chorus that turned the place inside out. When the madness stopped the other dead body Benedict had stuffed under the bed was blown apart. They sprayed the entire room blood red *Jackson Pollock* style getting it all over their armor. The lead Shocktroop looked frantically through the gory mess for signs of any other bodies, but saw only pieces of the one.

They sprinted back into the hall searching in desperate fashion when the other Shocktroop alerted his leader that he had just seen their targets fleeing around one pf the corners.

When the two Shocktroops had appeared at the end of the hall Nicky left the cop looking clown to deal with them. When Benedict had started shooting at them he and Lotus ran back into the hotel room then quickly made their way through the door that led into the adjoining room.

The second door behind it had been locked from the other side so, Nicky had to put a bullet into the lock then swiftly kicked it open. Neatly closing the doors behind them to mask their escape.

The second room was empty and Nicky knew when he heard the armored guys step inside room 777 looking for them that the loud high pitched humming and exploding debris was their cue. He and Lotus ran back out of the room and down the hallway. That's when they were spotted. They made it to the corner as they heard the *Shockwave* sonic boom behind them tearing the wall to shreds.

The concussion of the blast was so powerful it knocked Lotus into the opposite wall. Nicky had to quickly yank her back to her feet, "Come on, I ain't gone leave you here," he promised dragging her to her feet unsteadily down the hall. Luckily they made it around another corner just in time to hear the *Shockwave* humming again from behind. More chunks of drywall and plaster flew in their direction as the pulse rifle missed them. Nicky continued to run still pulling Lotus by her thin wrist until they ultimately reached set of double door that read, 'Maintenance Only'

Entering the small room they saw that it was filled with large industrial equipment and more importantly it had what Nicky had hoped for a freight-elevator that led to the basement. Nicky lifted up the roll up gate to the elevator as they both quickly hopped on board.

The Shocktroop that had fired the blast that knocked Lotus into the wall didn't see what he'd done, but he knew that he saw their targets turn the corner. Giving the force of their weapons, he knew he had to have at least caught one of them in the blast.

They were running after their targets, but the bulky armor was heavy and they were having their troubles keeping pace with them. When they got to the corner no one was there, but the second Shocktroop did however see the Asian girls shoe. Picking it up he announced,
"They are close," his voice a muffled Russian accent coming through the visor. When they finally made it into the maintenance room the large elevator was grinding its way towards the basement.

The lead Shocktroop lifted the gate and looked down the shaft at the slow moving lowering lift, then took up aim at the cables, "Die, *Yankee*,"
The hum of the *Shockwave* was followed by a loud snap from the cables as they gave into the force of the beam instantaneously,
"*Da*, this is how we bury Americans, yes?" he stated turning to his comrade who after looking down the dark shaft agreed with him.

The freight-elevator was already too many floors down for them to hear the weapon humming over the screeching metal. He hoped that they'd make it to the basement before they caught up to them. So when the elevator cable snapped it came as a completely horrifying surprise. Their speed increased rapidly as the freight dropped.

Lotus began clinging to Nicky in sheer terror, "Oh my, God we're going to die!" Nicky held her tightly in his arms and for the first time found himself honestly worried since he had met her. Being in a gunfight, he always knew he had a chance. As long as he had a bullet he had a shot, but this was totally out of his control, this *was* in the hands of fate. As the elevator plummeted Lotus looked in Nicky's eyes then begged him, "Kiss me,"

As Nicky leaned in to kiss her the emergency breaks squealed to life as the freight began to slow down, but it wasn't happening fast enough. They still had plenty of momentum and when they reached the basement they landed with a crash that threw them both to the floor hard. Silence followed the crashing of steel and screeching of brakes as Lotus coughed them moaned. Her leg was badly bruised from the impact.

"You okay?" Nicky asked weakly in the darkness.
"I..." she coughed a little, "Think so," Lotus groaned,
"Come on, we'll get out through the hatch. Here grab onto my shoulders..." he reached into the blackness and took her soft hand lifting her to her feet "You ready?" Lotus had to get her equilibrium first, after a few more moments she was. She crawled onto his back and eventually his shoulders then began fiddling with the elevator hatch sliding it to one side. Reaching out she pulled herself up and out of the smashed death box. She reached back down. Nicky reached up to catch Lotus' hand and was surprised by how effortlessly she helped pull him out. He looked at her in wonder for a second then spoke,
"Can you walk okay?" Lotus jumped down from the top of the busted freight elevator limping a few steps. She looked back up at him then playfully said, "I think you better carry me,"
 Nicky leaped down then scooped Lotus up into his arms slowly stepping off into the darkness.
A light was coming through a door cracked a little ways down and when Nicky opened it he saw that they were now in one of the underground parking lots, "We need some fresh wheels. Something low key like a… a,"

Lotus was silent then she burst out,
"A, this!" Nicky stopped and turned to see her
pointing at a *BMW* motorcycle,
"A bike... you serious...?
"Why not... a bike?" she shot back,
"Lower me down," Nicky lowered Lotus who
immediately got onto the motorcycle pulling out
her hair pin lock pick. Within a matter of seconds
the *BMW* roared to life and was ready to roll,
"Ready?" Lotus asked revving the throttle a few
times smiling at him. Nicky frowned back at her,
"What are you talking about, slide back,"
"I'm talking about you... you can't drive and shoot,
can you?" Nicky stared at her sweet face and was
fuming inside. Not only was he now on the run
potentially for murder, but her so called mystery
buyer turned out to be bullshit. He wanted to
blame himself for even getting involved with her,
but found himself taking it all out on Lotus,
 "I don't fuckin' believe you. We got half the city
trying to kill us and you want to play games *now!*"
"Fine, then you drive, but I told you I've never
shot anybody before,"
"First time for everything, sweetheart,"
"Yeah well, everybody can't just be a killer as easy
as you can,"
"So what you saying, I'm a murderer?"

Lotus held Nicky's' hard gaze then breathed out, "No... I'm not... and what about you?"

"What about me?"

"You blame me for all this, don't you...?"

Nicky wanted to say yes, it was just his New York attitude, but he didn't want to hurt her feelings right now. He did however tell himself when the time was right he would give her a proper ass chewing, "Just go ahead and admit it you're pissed at me," she rationalized,

"Admit what? That my whole world's been a one way ticket to shit since you came into my life. Or what, that I knew you were full of shit and there is no buyer... is that what you *want* to hear?"

"Yes," Lotus delivered her answer with an honest face. Nicky stared at her for a moment then told her, "You drive... I'll shoot,"

The *BMW* zoomed out from the underground parking garage as Lotus handled the luxury bike gracefully. Nicky was seated with his back to hers holding the reloaded Beretta low as he searched to see if they had any tails,

"Where'd you learn to drive?" he asked curiously as Lotus weaved the *BMW* through the busy late-nite Las Vegas traffic,

"Japan,"

On the street police sirens were heard coming from all over the city and heading in the direction of the *Casino Triple 7* where the Shocktroops were still causing unearthly havoc and death. Explosions went off to their rear as Police cars were blown apart by the escaping Shocktroopers near the Triple 7s' entrance.

"What about this place?" Lotus drove the motorcycle into a motel about twenty miles away from the all the chaos going on back in the city, "It's fine, just park around the back though," Nicky replied. He was sitting face forward on the bike now with his arms wrapped around Lotus waist. She pulled the *BMW* in the parking lot behind the building. Turning the ignition off Nicky helped her balance the bike,
"So, you call that a *honeymoon*?" she teased getting off the bike first. Nicky scanned the parking it was pass midnight and except for a few well lit up spots there was only darkness to be found,
"Go get us a room, I'll make sure nobody followed us," he said pulling out the pistol. Lotus looked to Nicky reading the frustration on his face. She was starting to feel like their brief romance was coming to an abrupt end. Her feelings for Nicky had grown immensely since making love with him and

she could only hope that he felt the same.

Her love life over the past year had consisted of cruel sex with a fat sadistic brute. Holding on to the feelings she felt was more crucial to Lotus than anything else, the diamonds, everything. She didn't want to let on too much at that moment for fear of pushing Nicky away, but she knew the time would come when she would have to tell him her true feelings.

The man standing at the hotel counter wore thick glasses that made his eyes look very huge as he stared at Lotus, "You coming from of a cocktail party or something?" The burly man awkwardly asked. Lotus just shook her head then handed the large man a hundred dollar bill,

"A room please,"

"Sure thing..." Taking the money he asked,

"How many beds?" Lotus looked back into the parking lot then put up two fingers.

The small motel room was crude, unkempt and disgusting. Nicky even swore that he had seen a cockroach crawling up under the mini fridge. He slammed the gym bag full of guns on the table then unzipped it, methodically checking the magazine of each one. Lotus shut the door then clicked the TV on looking for a news station. When she found one she plopped down onto one of the beds, turning the sound up with the remote. "*Daaamn*," she sang as she watched the live footage of the chaos going on near the Strip.

Nicky pulled a chrome *Desert Eagle* .50AE from the bag then cautiously moved toward the window. Peeking through the curtains he searched the dark parking lot for any movement, "Is anything good on?" Lotus asked mockingly. "Shhh! I think I see somebody com..." Nicky's' last word was cut off by a loud knock on the motel door. He turned to Lotus who was staring at the door with concern, "*Get over here,*" Nicky whispered as he aimed the *Desert Eagle* through the peep hole, "*Boy*, if you don't put that damn *thang* away..." A familiar woman's voice rang through the door like a watchful mother. The order was followed up by a scolding, "Niccolo?!"

Lowering the *Desert Eagle,* looking through the peep hole Nicky said, "I don't believe it... it's the psycho chic from the airport," Morganna cleared her throat announcing,

"I'm still waiting for you to open up this, *damn* door."
"Let her in already," Lotus insisted then slid the chain lock, opening the door as The Mystical Mistress Morganna walked into their motel room. Nicky kept his gun trained on Morganna from the moment she crossed the threshold. To him her

finding them all the way out in the middle of the desert after nearly getting their heads blown off was no coincidence,

"Well well well...look at who it is...," Nicky flickered his fingers in the air in a tickling motion.,

"It's the Ms. Tickle me *Elmo, bitch.."* he snapped making over exaggerated hand gestures as he glared at the high, not mighty just high, TV psychic. The final word was delivered with a hint of rage that Nicky had a difficult time concealing,

"Bitch...?" Morganna fumed, "Ya lucky I don't slap that gun down your throat, *child*..." she warned.

His insult was hurtful. She was only there to help them, but she knew exactly how many times they had nearly been killed so she decided to forgive him this time, "Now you'd betta watch ya mouth, Niccolo, *y'hear* me?"

"Don't call me that," Nicky threatened,

"Anyway..." she rolled her eyes at Nicky then winked at Lotus adding, "It didn't come to me until I boarded the plane..."

"Bullshit," Nicky interrupted,

"Boy, if you don't let me finish..." she gave Nicky a menacing glance then added, "It wasn't supposed to be the *Casino Triple 7*... It was the *Hospital Simple 7th Heaven,"*

"Wait a minute... how do you know about all that?" Morganna answered his question with a silent, confident squint that told him knew how. Nicky blinked, "*Riiight*... so you're trying to tell me we were supposed to figure all that out from smoking a joint? You for real lady, seriously how many of them joints you smoke on the way over here?"

"Shut up," Lotus whispered,

"Really, I really want to know... what the hell are you getting out of all of this?" Nicky waited for a semi honest answer from her,

"You know what, none of that even matters now,"

"Listen to her," Lotus advised to Nicky who turned to her and snapped,

"*You*... stay out of this, remember you still on punishment. So tell me Ms. Cleo, why not?"

"Because, no matter what I tell you now it won't change the fact that the two of you are still going to be in this situation together and the two of you, still have a choice to make," Morganna warned.

Chapter 8

When Nicky and Lotus walked into the fast food restaurant parking lot of the little well known burger joint with the *Jack in the Box* on the roof they saw that that the place was still open during the late hours. What had brought them here wasn't the food. The '*Hospital Simple 7th Heaven*' was right behind it. There was an ambulance parked in the back near the alley, so Nicky took this opportunity to make his introduction from the rear.

The guys inside the EMS where busy chowing down on some pan fried beef and cheese when a huge hand gun was stuffed inside the ambulance through the driver side window. Eddie Valentine swallowed the chunks of food in his mouth when he saw the *Desert Eagle.* He attempted to speak, "Whh ymm wmnt?" Eddies' words were muffled from food and fear. Nicky put up his free hand saying,
"Chew first, then swallow... then talk,"
Eddie blinked, then he began chewing his food into much smaller portions before swallowing it.

"Good boy," Nicky commented as if the scared man was a circus show dog doing a trick. Eddie frowned at him when Nicky told him to,
"Take a drink, wash it down,"
After he took a sip of his Orange *Crush* Eddie put the beverage back into the cup holder before looking to the kid with the handgun for more directions. This time when he spoke his words were clear,
"What's this all about?"
"Don't worry we're not gon' hurt you guys or nothing, thing is... we just need to borrow your truck," Nicky smiled at them easing their fears a little. Relief showed on the E.M.T.s' faces up until Lotus added,
"*Oh*, and we need your clothes too,"
The men looked at each other, then Eddie asked,
"What are you two into?"
"Trust me, bro... you *don't* want to know... "
Behind the EMS Nicky made the techs open the back door then followed them both inside. After they took off their jumpsuits Nicky tossed one of them to Lotus who rolled her dress up to her hips, then slid the jumpsuit on one leg at a time. When she finished putting it on Nicky grabbed the other uniform them put it on,
"How I look?" Lotus asked.
Nicky looked her from head to toe, "Like trouble...

come on help me *tie'em* up."

"This really necessary man, *please*," Eddie begged.
"Nothing personal, we'll let somebody know
where you guys are at,"
They drove the ambulance into the Hospitals
underground entrance. Nicky was behind the
wheel. The loading area was quiet and despite the
obvious camera that was posted high above the
entrance no other eyes were down there.
Nicky parked the ambulance in one of the
emergency spots then slammed it into park,
"Let's go."
"Am I off punishment?" Lotus pried.
Nicky responded by getting out and slamming his
door. Nicky walked swiftly into an entrance that
led down into the hospitals basement. Lotus
swiftly jogged up next to him,
"Is this how you treat your *wife*?" she cracked.
Nicky wasn't in a playful mood any longer. Being
wanted across the US and endlessly being hunted
by strong-arms had ran its toll on the young man,
"Shhhh, keep quiet..."
Lotus frowned at his reply as she scanned the area
up ahead,
"Were in a... *hospital*," Nicky delivered the line
with a little bit of humorous tone and a slight grin.

The seventh floor was silent as the elevator doors creaked open. Nicky looked to his left where he saw a lone receptionist sitting at her desk scrolling through her cell phone, "This way." he whispered.

Going in the opposite direction Nicky began checking the numbers on the doors. The room was supposedly the same number as the hotels. When they reached their destination Nicky turned to look at Lotus in the oversize EMT uniform and had to question his own sanity.

Now here he was thousands of miles away from home, wanted for questioning for countless bodies left across American soil, standing in a Las Vegas hospital armed with a gun, looking for a mystery buyer and not to mention he got all this from a TV psychic. One thing was certain at this point, he couldn't go back so he went forward and opened the door.

The first bed was empty. The curtain was drawn between the second bed and the first. Creeping pass the drapery they saw an old man lying under the covers there. The TV was on a news channel broadcasting more footage on the Casino shootout, but the old man's eyes were closed. Lotus looked at the old man then turned to Nicky only to see absolute shock written across his face, "*What*, what's wrong?"

Nicky was too stunned to respond to her.

The face in the bed was all too familiar to him because he had seen it since he was a toddler. It belonged to a man responsible for so many good things in his family's life,

"Lucky?"

Nicky turned to Lotus who was shaking his arm roughly. Lotus waited for him to say something as she watched Nicky pick up the chart at the foot of the bed then scan it. He finally answered her,

"He's my grandfath..." A silenced shot cracked as Nicky's right shoulder exploded with a burning sensation. Overwhelmed from the pain he dropped the *Desert Eagle* to the floor grabbing for his bleeding shoulder,

"Stings don't it...?" asked Giuseppe Cigarilli, b/k/a Don Vittolo a/k/a Nicky's grandfather, "Well don't just stand there, sweetie, the chart... he's bleeding all over it," The Don commented. Lotus looked at Nicky then back to his grandfather. A smoking hole could be seen in the white sheets where the bullet had burned its way through,

"Well... what are you waiting for...?" Don Vittolo snapped impatiently. Lotus slowly began to kneel down picking up the chart, dropping it onto his food tray, "Good girl, now... where is it?"

He interrogated,

"Why did you just shoot your own grandson?" she asked in bewilderment.

"He got to toughen up someday. Now, no more questions, give it here, *now…!*" Lifting his right arm from under the covers he revealed a GLOCK 17 with an AAC suppressor fitted on the barrel aiming it directly at Nicky's face.

"So that's what this is... all this time, you were a part of the... *Mafia*?" Nicky grunted the question out through his pain,

"What's left of it," Lotus snapped sarcastically,

"*Wroooong…* and I ain't just *part* of... I *am* the Mafia... the King of the Volcano,"

"And my dad?" Nicky wondered aloud,

"Well, what can I say about him accept... he was fucking up the entire family. Now that was the last one, next time either of you speak it *betta* be about the jewelry,"

The silence that followed on only infuriated the Don causing him to lift his gun a fraction,

"Okay, the count of three. One... two... three *oooooh..* now there's a piece..."

Lotus pulled the small platinum *Derringer* with the rare pink diamonds aiming it at the Dons' face, "*Damn*, ain't she a beaut...," The Don smiled at Nicky telling him, "She ain't half bad either *huh...?*" he winked at Lotus then said. "A girl after my own heart, I tell you, if only I was forty years younger. You want to thank me now for her now or what?"

Nicky's painful expression was abruptly mixed with confusion, "That's right... how do you think she got to you? Did you even take the time to examine that gun she brought you?" The Don asked. Nicky thought back to that fateful meeting back at the gun store realizing he didn't, he didn't have time too, "That's right, I got a man in that fat sushi eating pricks organization reporting any and everything he finds out right back to me..."

The Don looked to Lotus then added,

"Well, I *had* one,"

"But, that was Koji gun," Now it was Lotus' turn to look confused.

"Like I said... I had one. Okay end of the history lesson, give it here,"

Lotus didn't budge. A knock on the door alerted everyone's attention towards that direction. At that moment Nicky sensed a change and took advantage leaping onto the bed grabbing a hold of the silenced pistol. His grandfather was old and in normal circumstances Nicky would have easily overpowered him, but the gunshot wound had sapped his strength and he was struggling to hold onto the weapon as it swung in Lotus' direction.

The door to the room squeaked opened as a short brown skinned lady dressed in a full nurses uniform entered the hospital room pulling a cart that was carrying his dinner tray on top of it.

"Are we ready for our sponge bath now, Mr. Cigarilli?" she asked pulling the cart inside with her back facing them all. Lotus was still standing at the foot of the bed aiming the Derringer at the Don, so when the nurse turned to see the little Asian girl with the sparkling gun in her hand pointing at one of her patients she screamed at the top of her lungs setting of a chain of devastating events.

First the silenced pistol went off catching the nurse in her thigh and knocking her off of her feet. Next the Don reached over and dug his hand into Nicky's' bullet wound, but he wasn't trying to help him remove it. The slightest movements of his index finger was followed by excruciating pain that forced Nicky to release his grip on the GLOCK. With the gun now free the Don set his sights on Lotus when. 'POP!'
The silence that followed the loud sound was awfully awkward. Nicky looked down at his grandfather's corpse. A bloody hole was in the center of his forehead, but his eyes were still open staring back at him. Nicky didn't know what to feel, the man had just tried to kill him, but before tonight he had been the most important man in his and his family's lives since his father died. It was almost surreal then the nurse's loud screams returned bringing reality back with them.

Nicky quickly dismissed any emotion as the pain shot his mind back to the situation they were in, "Come on... let's get... out of here," his words were rough grunts that snapped Lotus from her daze. They reached the door when the heard something clatter to the floor from the dead man's bed. Lotus peered behind the curtain to see a cell phone face down on the floor, "Grab it," Nicky directed. She picked it up, the screen was cracked. She checked it to make sure that it still worked, then the two of them were gone.

Outside of the hospital the parking lot was quiet. A single security car was slowly patrolling an area just southwest to where they were now hiding behind a *Ford Explorer*. In the distance more sirens could be heard as if it had become a part of the soundtrack to their lives, "Come on," Nicky whispered leading her back around the bed of a Ford F1-50 when the sound of the handgun chambering a live round came just a few inches in front of Nicky's.

Looking up he saw the sour puss of the whiny old guy from the 7th floor back at the *Triple* 7 hotel Now Nicky knew this guy was a cop, he had to be. "Alone at last, you know you two left a nasty helping of shit back there. They'll be sorting out the bodies for weeks...," Benedict chuckled a little then added,

"Why don't you come with me, I got a much nicer ride for you?" he led them to a navy blue *Ford Crown Victoria*. Opening the rear passenger side door for them to get in Benedict removed the purse from Lotus' arm, "I'll take that,"

The *Smith & Wesson* No.29 44 Magnum was now directly between Nicky's eyes, "Now you... the toys," Nicky held Benedict's hard gaze for along moment until the intense pain shooting through his shoulder made him wince,

"Let's go cupcake!" Benedict was growing agitated and it was visibly showing in his face which appeared even more frowned up than usual. Nicky handed him the *Desert Eagle*,

"Good *Guinea*... now in you go,"

After slamming the door Benedict began to whistle, *'We're in the money'* When he got to the driver's door his whistling stopped abruptly as a swift kick caught him square in the jaw dropping him hard to the ground. Groaning in pain he looked up holding the side of his jaw to see the evil expression of the face of Johnny Flash, Boss Itoro number one assassin,

"*You*... you sushi son of a bitch! I'll."

A single shot from Johnny's CZ 97 ended the policeman threats. Johnny didn't even waste time to check the body, instead kicking it off to the side.

He jumped in the car without even looking at Nicky or Lotus when she blurted out his name, "Johnny?!"

"You know him?" Nicky asked quietly.

"Yeah, he's Yakuza... believe me, you *don't* want to piss him off," Johnny peeked back at Nicky through the rear view mirror flashing a sinister smile at him. He held his gaze until finally lighting up a cigarette. Putting the car in drive he eased the unmarked squad car out onto the dark avenue. The road ahead was clear when Johnny decided to finally flip the headlights on. Up until now he had basically played the shadows waiting for either Benedict to drop a clue or find the buyer before anyone else did. Nonetheless his patience had paid off and Boss Itoro was sure to reward him greatly for his role in retrieving his *Master's* mistress and his diamonds. Lotus turned to Nicky,

"Look... I just want to say... I'm sorry for all this shit... I never thought it would get this far... do you *think*... you could ever forgive me?" Nicky heard the sincerity in Lotus' request, almost as if she were repenting to a Pentecostal priest, "We ain't dead yet," Nicky grunted loud enough so Johnny could hear him. Johnny looked into the rear view pass Nicky into the blinding high beams coming from behind them. The bright lights were speeding up. Suddenly a black *Hummer*-H1 pulled alongside the *Crown Victoria* then the window rolled down. The arm that came out of it had one of the infamous *Shockwaves* in it as the man attempted to one hand the powerful weapon. He managed to squeeze out an electrified beam that blew the road and their front wheel apart. Johnny however was not about to give in to defeat. No... never, for he was *Bushido*. Whipping his CZ 97 out with practiced speed he returned fire hitting the weapon near the trigger clipping the guy's hand. The ridiculously expensive weapon smashed onto the ground sending pieces of scrap metal scattering as the bright neon lights on the weapon died out. Another shot hit his arm. He jerked it back inside from the bullets impact. Johnny cursed in Japanese, "*Anata o fakku!*"

The *Crown Victoria* was driving on one of ts axles now, grinding deep grooves into the roadway. Sparks flew along the asphalt as the Yakuza mobster held the wobbling wheel steady in his hands. Blinding lights pinned the windshield forcing him to bring the car to a screeching halt. Before he could even get the car in park combat black-suited commandos were all around the *Crown Victoria* and all were pointing *Shockwaves,* "Get them out of there now!" The man called T.R.I.G.G.E.R. yelled. The rear door was ripped open by the commandos as Lotus was snatched out screaming and kicking.. One brute threw her over one of his shoulder like a sack of potatoes ignoring her punches, pinches and bites. Nicky slid out on his own and was thrown up roughly up against the side of the *Hummer* then frisked. "He's clean,"

T.R.I.G.G.E.R. nodded his approval to the commando then patted the young man on his back with his good hand. Whipping out his side arm he aimed it at Nicky's face, then fired a shot off into the sky, "I ought to blow your fucking head off right now..." T.R.I.G.G.E.R. threatened then stuck the hot mussel of his *Colt* M1911 into Nicky's gunshot wound painfully digging it into his flesh. The anguish on the young man's face spread the cruel man's lips wickedly in a cold smile, then he added, "but I think I want you to see something first,"

Nicky, Lotus and Johnny Flash were tied up in the back of one of the military vehicles with two guns in their faces. They had been driving for most of the night and it was getting close to dawn somewhere on that little dirt road to nowhere they'd been convoying down for dozens of miles now. Surprisingly the lead vehicle, which they just happened to be inside of suddenly stopped as T.R.I.G.G.E.R. announced, "We're here."

Here... was a place that time had long forgotten, the little town of Gold Bluff, Nevada was now nothing but a haunted ghost town. The winds whistled a thousand stories as the military convoy finally parked on a dirt road that once served as the main road into this little settlement. Of course that had been once upon a time yesteryear when the place was still home to a very rich gold mine. The ruins of a fire station and saloon were evident despite the ravage of time, rain and sand,

"Out!" T.R.I.G.G.E.R. barked as the soldiers in the back removed Nicky slamming him to the ground. He landed directly on his bloody shoulder wound. Despite Nicky's' groans of pain the black-suited commandos roughly drug him around the corner of an old rotted wooden building that had probably been a church at one point. Lotus was escorted over in the same direction, but Johnny Flash however didn't come along so willingly. When his feet touched ground he immediately chopped the man next to him in the throat leaving him gagging for oxygen. Another man coming from behind wrapped his massive arms around the prisoner who threw his head back into his nose with bone cracking force. The crimson mustache the mercenary now wore was proof to the fact. His release of the Yakuza assassin would only lead to more punishment for his brothers in arms until finally a soldier took up aim with a prototype weapon that fired a weighted net that slammed Johnny to the dirt like wild game. Five soldiers surrounded him as Johnny struggled to free himself. The men took turns viciously jabbing him with long high powered stun guns, the volts temporarily neutralizing the hotheaded assassin, When Nicky was finally led to T.R.I.G.G.E.R. he saw that the man was still wearing those same sunglasses he wore the first time they met, chomping on a fresh *Cuban* cigar. Nicky looked at the man's hand, he could still hear faint echoes in his head of the man's screams when he had been forced to commit surgery and amputate. It had been replaced with an advanced prosthesis, the remarkable artificial limb was the best tax money could buy, he was also wearing black gloves over it so to Nicky's eyes it almost looked like the mans hand had miraculously grown back,

"I believe I owe you something..." T.R.I.G.G.E.R. reminded Nicky aiming a strange looking gun in his face. It was the size of a large caliber pistol with a small oval silencer like device attached to the barrel. T.R.I.G.G.E.R.s thumb clicked a switch along the slide, causing bright neon lights to run all over the guns frames as the oval silencer slowly opened up revealing a neon glowing mini dish similar to the ones on the rifle size *Shockwaves,*

"*Y'know...* you all should consider yourselves really lucky, I mean here you are getting ready to leave your mark on US History... *and* all over this desert..." T.R.I.G.G.E.R. chuckled a little before continuing, "by being the first ones to die today... with the weapons of tomorrow,"

Nicky stared into the mini dish getting slightly hypnotized by the dancing neon lights inside of it. T.R.I.G.G.E.R. smiled at him cruelly behind the impressive weapon then clicked the button on the slide. The lights died out as the mini dish closed, "*Y'know* as an American I have to say that I am damn proud of this country..." T.R.I.G.G.E.R. was speaking in a conversational tone, he began walking as he continued, "I'm speaking in terms of execution... I mean *hell*, now we don't even have to leave HQ. Push one button and... Boom! Five thousand degrees of death. Then of course you got these," T.R.I.G.G.E.R. held up the *Shockpistol,* "You like? It's just as powerful as its' big brother, but a lot more concealable. But like I always say... you just can't beat a classic," Looking up at the old platform T.R.I.G.G.E.R. smirked at the noose hanging over the trap door, "So, kid, which way you want it, quick...," T.R.I.G.G.E.R. asked as he lifted the *Shockpistol,* "Or slow?" aiming the weapon up at the noose then back down at Nicky. Nicky watched the man's face beam with a victorious icy smile that quickly began to melt away. The smile on T.R.I.G.G.E.R.s' face became nonexistent as the sound of helicopter blades were heard moving in fast somewhere off in the distance, coming in from the south. The familiar sound put all the commandos on high alert as T.R.I.G.G.E.R. gave hand signals for some of his men to take cover in firing positions. The rest of his commandos remained with him, guarding their prisoners. T.R.I.G.G.E.R. looked to the distant sky nervously. He was already on enough pain killers to numb a brontosaurus and was now having a slight case of paranoia. Who the hell knew where they were?

That question was answered as a *Sirkorsky Black Hawk* ML -60 DAP swooped down across the sky. The aircraft came in across the skyline like some angry mid-evil dragon, but instead of breathing fire it spat 30-mm rounds from a devastating M230 Chain Gun. A rocket sped into an abandoned garage where two mercenaries had been safely crouched. The explosion sent shrapnel and wood slivers into the men leaving only bloody rag dolls left in the fiery wake.

Nicky and Lotus took this opportunity to make an escape running behind the church they were standing next to. One of the commandos saw the movement then spun firing his *Shockwave* at them.

The church was obliterated as half of the entire back wall was punched open into a million slivers of old wood. Moving in for his kill he took up aim when he saw Lotus on the ground on top of Nicky. The two of them had been dropped from the concussive force. He aimed the *Shockwave* down at them slowly wrapping his finger around the trigger when, he heard,
"Scatter!"
The panicked order coming from his superior startled the commando. Caught him off guard he looked up in a rush to see the *Black Hawk* making a second pass, its mini guns steady blazing death.

  T.R.I.G.G.E.R. shouted the command as he ran for one of those empty structures dismissing the prisoners and focusing now only on survival. Three of his men opened fire with the *Shockwaves* but were chopped to pieces by the *Black Hawks* bullets. However not before successfully taking the war bird down, sending it smashing into a brilliant hill side explosion.
    T.R.I.G.G.E.R. looked down to see that the weighted prototype net was now empty. It appeared that their other Asian prisoner had somehow miraculously pulled a Harry Houdini. "Find 'em, kill 'em!" T.R.I.G.G.E.R. ordered as he ran in the opposite direction for the main road.

When the helicopter was shot down Nicky and Lotus took advantage of the commandos confusion running in the direction of the old gold mines. The men were too busy fighting for their life, ignoring them as they kept firing as the second helicopter swooping in before they also were dropped from the Black Hawks lethal lead storm.

They were almost near the hill that led to the mines entrance, when Nicky suddenly dropped from pain and blood loss, "Oh no you don't, you get your ass up!" Lotus screamed pulling at his arm in the same way he had yanked on hers so many times before, "Come... on!" she repeated marching him forward.

"Forget about it... just, just get out of here, okay?" Nicky complained.

"And leave my lucky charm. *Un-uh,* I don't think so..." This time she put some strength into it and lifted Nicky to his feet,

"Come on lover boy, move your ass!"

T.R.I.G.G.E.R. and his remaining mercenaries were met on the main road by MR. A.K. and his own convoy of expensive urbanized military vehicles, *Knight VXs* to be exact,

"What the hell you think you're doing, you dumb *Rusky son of a bitch*?!" T.R.I.G.G.E.R. barked.

Mr. A.K.'s expression was cold and emotionless as he aimed his own *Shockwave* in their allies' direction, "My deepest apologies, comrade, but as we are all very much aware orders are to be followed no matter how distasteful they may be..." Mr. A.K's explained in a thick accent. The order to fire that followed was giving in his native tongue.

The American commandos didn't stand a chance, the *Shockwaves* ripped them apart like dandelions being plucked by the wind or better still like blood filled balloons, popping legs, arms and even heads in torn, ragged, crimson soaked chunks. T.RI.G.G.E.R. found himself alone staring into the eyes of his former ally and soon to be killer,

"I'll see you in Hell," T.R.I.G.G.E.R. warned the foreign traitor,

"*Da*... that is what I love about Americans, they always know the right thing to say, *but* unfortunately for you, comrade, this is *not* a movie," The *Shockwave* hummed to life sending its annihilating electrified charge into T.R.I.G.G.E.R.s head bursting it wide open with the impact of a sledgehammer through an eggplant. What served as the remains of the man's head could have easily been mistaken for road kill.

Mr. A.K. turned to one of his men and smiled at the former Black Ops leader's corpse when another one of his Spetsnaz soldiers pointed toward a mine off in the distance.

"There!" the man hollered aiming his *Shockwave* at Nicky and Lotus who were slowly headed for the mines entrance. Mr. A.K. put up a hand signaling the soldier to lower his weapon, then aimed his own weapon at the entrance and fired.

Lotus dragged Nicky inside the cave when the tunnel opening surprisingly collapsed on top of the two of them, pinning them underneath a mass of dirt and rock. The interior of the cave was now pitch black and the silence that followed the cave-in left little hope that anyone had survived. Mr. A.K. was pleased at the sight he saw, finally the one responsible for his brothers untimely death was now himself buried... alive hopefully he thought, hoping to prolong the man's suffering, "*Da*, that is how we bury Americans, yes?" His Spetsnaz soldiers all nodded their agreement then followed their comrade General back toward their vehicles. After searching the grounds of the ghost town for more survivors the military convoy soon disappeared off into the bright Nevada sun.

Inside of the mine darkness filled the void of silence. Nicky was buried alive in the blasted rubble and barely conscious. Caked blood and dirt covered his face as he reached through feeling for Lotus... nothing. The silence was suddenly broken by a cell phone ringtone to the theme of the *Godfather* movies. Nicky fumbled through the dirt searching, searching... where the hell was it?

"Hello...?" Lotus' voice was small in the darkness. Nicky just listened as her voice became a little bit louder, "Yeah we got it, you got the money?"

It was him, the mystery man everyone was killing and dying to meet out here in this deadly desert.

"Okay, I'll call you back in one hour," Lotus ended the call then heard.

"*Yooo!*"

Lotus snapped her head in the direction of Nicky's' muffled voice as she began clawing at the rocks and dirt. Using the cell phone for light she continued frantically. Hands full of dirt produced no signs of hope then abruptly her wrist was grabbed in a tight all too familiar way. She pulled at Nicky's' arm until his head popped through the soil. Lotus helped him out. Soon as Nicky crawled to his feet he cracked,

"Nice of you to tell me that you wasn't *dead*."

"I was on the phone,"

"I heard, so, what's up?"

"He's ready to meet us?"

"He?"

"Yeah, the buyer."

"So, he got the *money*?"

"Yes, at least he says he does..."

Nicky knew what that meant, they were going to need a little 9mm insurance, "Shouldn't we be worrying about something else right now?"

"What?"

"Like getting out of here before we suffocate?"

"Give me the light," Nicky took the cell phone from her hand, exploring further off into the mine. Lotus wrapped her arm around Nicky as they moved further off into the cave,

"At least we're together," Lotus whispered. Nicky refused to give up, but blood lost and pain from his gunshot wound had left his arm numb and he was now running on pure adrenaline. They walked into a mine shaft that had once flourished with clusters of golden nuggets,

"Over there!"

Nicky looked in the direction Lotus tapped him towards. There, was a thin stream of light coming in like a slice of Heaven, "*Yes!*" Nicky headed for the direction of the sunlight, '*like a suicidal vampire*' he held the cell up to the light where he saw salvation in the form of a rotten old wooden ladder that they both climbed to the surface.

The trap door to the mine opened as bright Nevada sunshine welcomed them back to civilization. Nicky made it out first then he helped Lotus up, "Thanks..." walking over to the edge, scanning the valley below, she awkwardly asked, "Did you see what happened to Johnny?" "Nope, too busy keeping us alive," Lotus turned to face Nicky, walking back up to him smiling, "You mean... I was *too* busy," Nicky was too weak to argue with her, "You win," "I know, come on let's get out of here. Maybe they left one of the trucks for us?" The Russians had made sure to leave no witnesses or evidence blowing up all the remaining trucks along with any surviving members of T.R.I.G.G.E.R.s' former team, so one thing was for sure, it was going to be a long walk back to Vegas. Walking through the ghost town they were greeted by the grisly sight of the aftermath of the hell storm they had just survived. The dirt was soaked with blood and littered with the bodies of the commandos, but there was no sign of Johnny Flash. Lotus stopped when she noticed something underneath some rubble, she picked it up handing Nicky the *Shockpistol*. He examined it, then quickly stuffed it down his pants leg. As they traveled under the hot Nevada desert sun Lotus carried Nicky with one of his arms spread over her slim shoulders. Amazingly she held him upright with little effort. At the time Nicky had lost too much blood to focus on that fact, but later he realized that his life had been entirely in her hands since leaving the hospital and at this point he owed her for saving his life, as much if not more than she owed him. And to top it all off carrying him so far and not complaining once. Those untrustworthy feelings Nicky first had when he first met her were now officially lost somewhere back there in that Nevada ghost-town. Nicky's thoughts were broken as a mysterious white stretched limo pulled up on the empty dirt road then slowed down to a crawl next to them. Nicky whipped out the *Shockpistol* aiming it at the rear window as it slowly slid down halfway,

"Buenos Dias, Amigo..."

It was the same Hispanic voice on the phone, Lotus thought. It was him. Lotus had heard the voice, but Nicky had never heard it before in his life. He held the *Shockpistol* steady feeling his fingers starting to tense, "My friend, there is no need for that... I am, the *Buyer*," The voice assured him. Nicky hesitated to lower the gun when he felt Lotus slowly pushing his arm down to his side, "Please, get in," the voice offered as the door cracked wide open for them to enter the limo.

Lotus got in first, then Nicky still holding the weapon followed her in. The man sitting in the back of the limo was dressed in a gold silk suit wearing an expensive pair of sunglasses with sparkling diamonds. The bright smile on his face almost competed with the man's jewelry. No one was in the back with them, which made Nicky feel a little more at ease. Nicky however wasn't putting his gun away, "So, may I see the merchandise?" The buyer asked. He was distinctly Mexican clean shaved and had a head full of thick dark hair. Lotus pulled the *Derringer* from under her dress then held it up. The jeweled one shot pistol glistened as the Buyer reached out to take the weapon.

Nicky lifted the *Shockpistol* at the Buyers' head, when the sound of a gun cocking reached his ears. He didn't see it, but he definitely felt the barrel pressing deep into his skull, "That is Edgar, my brother... he is very protective of me, now if you would just lower your gun, we can continue," The Buyer warned. Nicky's eyes shifted to the left before he reluctantly lowered the space age weapon. Edgar's gun was removed as well, "Good... now I suppose you would like to see the money...?" Lotus nodded to the buyer who picked up a large black case from the floor handing it over to Nicky, "Would you like to count it,

Amigo?"

"7 million?" Nicky rushed,

"That is 3.5 million. 7 million is the market value. "Where's the rest of it?" Lotus questioned looking from the Buyer to Nicky as the two men were now locked in an intense stare down,

"Edgar has the rest of it up front with him. Amigo you have a good woman there, I always say take care of your woman and your woman will take care of you," his strong, vibrant laughter quickly dissolved any tension left in the air as he slid another case full of money over to them,

"Would either of you like a drink?" the Buyer offered,

"I would..." Lotus confessed taking the glass of champagne the Buyer handed her as he poured from the gold bottle, "*Arigatou...* thank you,"

"You're welcome my dear,"

Nicky then asked, "Any more glasses?"

"Finish the bottle," the Buyer insisted.

Nicky took the *Cristal* champagne then turned the entire bottle upright as he set about drowning his pain in the golden liquid,

"I got to ask, how the hell did you find us all the way out here?" Nicky questioned.

"I admit I have known where you have been for the last five hours. I decided you must have been planning to make the exchange far from the city so I tracked your cellphone into the desert," the Buyer confessed.

"How did *you* do that?" Lotus asked determined to satisfy her own curiosity,

"Let us just say... I have important friends in very, very high places..." he pointed a finger to the roof, "Have you ever had *Cristal* before...?"

Nicky shook his head,

"How is it?" The Buyer inquired already knowing the answer,

"Right now, it taste *fuckin'* delicious,"

The Buyer smiled at him saying,

"Get used to it, nothing but the best... is there any particular place you two would like to be dropped off at, a hospital perhaps?"

"The closest strip club..." Lotus playfully suggested. The Buyer frowned a little at her response looking at Nicky's bloody shoulder, "Because, If I'm not mistaken... I still owe you a lap dance,"

"Don't you mean, the nearest wedding chapel?" Nicky asked turning to Lotus who smiled as she stood up then lowered herself onto Nicky's lap gyrating slowly to the soft music playing,

"I do," she purred. The Buyer's smile returned as he lifted a tiny remote control in his hand, which he used to turn the volume up as earthshaking club music came pounding out the speakers along

with colorful dancing disco lights that bounced all around them. The back seat of the limo lit up like the Las Vegas Strip on a Saturday night. Lotus wrapped her arms around Nicky's head leaning in close to his ear whispering,
"You still feeling, *lucky*?"
"Oh yeah... *always*,"
"Well, just wait until our honeymoon,"
This time Nicky smiled.

www.ingramcontent.com/pod-product-compliance
Lightning Source LLC
Chambersburg PA
CBHW020138180626
46810CB00004B/1613